FREE LOVE

By

Myah Lee

Dedicated to my firstborn with love.

CHAPTER 1

The pipe George had made for her was in a box kept by her on top of the refrigerator. "Whalebone," he said. She knew it was ivory, but was it from a whale? He carved it into a flower, knowing how much she loved flowers. Delicate petals held the pipe's bowl; long, lacey tendrils wrapped around the stem. She was the only one who had a pipe like this! After contemplating a minute or two, Jane padded over to the box and held it high above her head as she said, "This one's for you, Georgie, I love you."

From her antique match holder that hung near the stove, she took a wooden match and lit the candle she kept in the middle of the table, pulling it closer to her. It was a multi-colored taper candle, having an hour or so left to burn, stuck in a twine-wrapped wine bottle thickly covered in wax drippings of previous burnings.

It was a beautiful morning. Fall was beginning to show all her colors. Dewy dots on roses made them sparkle in the early morning sun. The air was crispy and fresh.

Big Brother and the Holding Company were on the radio, and she turned up the volume because Janis Joplin was 'outa-sight' in Jane's world. Loading her pipe with a small pinch of grass, she began to sing along, "...take – another – piece – of – my – heart – now- baby..."

At the old oak table where she sat every morning, Jane snuggled in Papa's comfy chair. She contemplated what lay ahead in the day. Since it was her day off, she wanted to shop for beads. Her little girl, DD, asked to make another beaded necklace after school. She liked to teach her six-year-old daughter crafts like Jane's own mother taught her many years ago... "Janie, don't eat the paste!" She remembered her mom telling her more than one time as they made funny animals together. Jane loved her mom's skill at smoothing the paste over a shiny balloon. She remembered not wanting to wait for it to dry so she could pop the balloon inside, laughing when she did. Then, discovering her mom's finished art was amazing in her little eyes. It made her heart feel good, too! Jane was adamant about passing this love and life on to her daughter. Now that she had one.

"... another – piece - of - my - heart ..." she continued to belt out the song with Janis.

Jane reached for another match, put it in the flame of the candle, and then lit her pipe. With one big inhale, she began to cough. "Good stuff," she mumbled to herself, "Wish George were here to share it with me." She closed her eyes and sighed deeply. Jane took another smaller inhale of the harsh smoke. She didn't cough this time, even though she held the smoke in her lungs for as long as she possibly could. George said that was the best way to get high.

Jane smiled as she gently rubbed the soft brown mohair on the side of the chair. With her head tilted to one side, she let her shoulders relax. Feeling the softness of Papa's chair, she ponders how lucky she is to have known her great-grandfather, and she knows that not many people have this privilege. Grandfathers are one thing, but usually, a great-grandfather has already passed when you're born. Her great-grandfather didn't pass away until she was 9 years old. A very well-respected citizen, Papa is what she called him. She admired Papa for his friendly ways. He spoke to every person he ever came across. If she was with him, he would always make her say hi, too. "No matter who they are, how they are or what they look like, we are all the same species. It'd be a shame not to communicate or, at leastways, smile." Papa

2

emphasized the need to be kind to everyone. Always whistling, Papa was a happy man. He taught Jane how to whistle when she was just four. In those younger days when Jane stayed at her grandma's house, she cuddled with Papa in this soft chair. He softly whistled soothing tunes, one after another, until they both fell asleep.

Memories of his after-shave bring the scent into her mind. She can smell it. Oh, how she misses her Papa, his hugs, and his constant love for her. After Papa passed away, little Janie was asked what she might want that belonged to him. At nine years old, she could only think of this old chair. It was a big chair, not a kitchen chair but an overstuffed easy chair. Her folks let her put it in her bedroom. She piled all her stuffed animals on the chair, making them comfortable, telling them Papa would let them sleep well. When she got older, Jane eventually had to keep the stuffing from falling out of the chair. She made patches out of an old pair of jeans that she sewed onto the arms of the chair, which were very badly worn. She patched the cigar burn her Papa put in the seat cushion, exaggerating all her colorful stitches to make the patches stand out loudly. Jane loves this cozy chair and the comforting feeling it gives her. She doesn't care how old and patched up it is; she will keep repairing it forever.

The nightgown she was still wearing this morning, tattered and well-worn, had more memories of her grandma, who died not too long after Papa. Jane kept it all these years because she's so sentimentally attached to it. The blue flowered fabric was getting so thin that she seldom wore it anymore, but last night was one of those occasions, one that she had anticipated, typical of the full moon when it was hard for her to sleep. Wearing the nightgown always made her feel snuggly and cozy, like warm cocoa in front of a hot fire, like the many nights she slept at her Grandma's house with Papa right there, sleeping in his own bedroom. She wore it for the peaceful comfort it gave her, and Jane swore it helped her sleep.

She takes another hit off the pipe and releases it slowly. Relaxation washes over Jane's body. Her arm drops to the soft side of the chair.

Strawberry blonde hair is held out of her face by a pale blue headband she had made. Two long braids framing her soft, round face were tied at the ends with ribbons. Jane wore violet and scarlet beads on a silver chain around her neck. She vowed to keep these beads on, close to her heart, for the rest of her life because her best friend George had made them just for her. Jane remembered those days as being some of the best times with the greatest memories of her life. George was her friend, her buddy, her flower giver, and the one who was a brother. He loved Jane in a purely natural way, with no rules. He was a Libra and kept life in balance. He looked upon her as his sister, not a little sister, but as a sister equal to himself, and Jane loved him for that. She loved George for so many reasons.

George liked to party hardy and smoke grass. But the one thing Jane didn't love, she really hated, was that he grew to like pills even more. He was very into downers. They did occasionally party together, but Jane didn't like the groggy feeling those pills gave her, so she didn't take them, although she did like the drunkenness. "To be drunk without wine," she would say about these red barbiturates.

She feels as if a weighted blanket is heavy over her shoulders. Tears run down her cheeks. Memories sometimes overwhelm Jane. The truth haunts her.

Jane misses George every day. She adores all of his memories. His picture is hung in every room of her cozy little house, cram-packed full of treasures. She had her favorite picture of George enlarged to poster size and hung it over the kitchen table, next to the 'Fuck Housework' poster. Most of all, she liked this picture of George on the beach because he

4

was laughing in it, almost to tears and looking at it always made her smile. George didn't want her to take his picture on that particular day, so he flipped her off and held it until she took the shot. It took her so long to focus because she was laughing so hard that his finger began to cramp in that 'bird' position, and he couldn't move it.

"That's what you get, buddy," Jane blurted out.

"No, Janie baby, that's what I DON'T get!" George said, laughing desperately.

His eyes filled with tears as he continued to laugh hard.

Worried his finger would be cramped in that position forever, he began to moan in pain. And then he laughed again, uncontrollably, all the while holding his finger, refusing to end the 'bird'.

Jane finally got the shot and fell back into the sand. They both laughed hysterically! Tears filled Jane's eyes, too, and they both held their stomachs in pain from laughing so hard. Every time they looked at each other, they laughed again. They laughed until they ran out of energy to laugh anymore, and George collapsed onto the beach, moaning in delight. Jane massaged his middle finger in her hands while she smiled controllably without laughing. The picture actually turned out to be a great poster. Waves in the background, with the water looking especially blue that day, made it dramatic. His 'bird-flipping' hand being held tightly by his other hand was as if he emphasized the f-you, and Jane thought it fit well next to the fuck housework poster.

These memories were good times, full of incredible fun and craziness. This summer day was one full of grass and foolish idiocy, a happy day to remember. Those days are only alive in Jane's memories now. And so is George. She still occasionally cries herself to sleep, thinking about him and how he was always there for her, no matter what. But where was she for him? Where was she when he desperately needed her?! Tears flooded Jane's eyes again. She shuffled over to the window, stared outside a while, and then returned to her chair.

After another hit of smoke, Jane began to feel better. Her body relaxed, and she felt peaceful again. She put her pipe away.

"When will I get over you, Georgie? Will I ever?"

She looked at his picture again and smiled, "Peace to you, Georgie, with the beautiful peace I feel right now." She sighed with a deep breath. "Now, lets both have a nice day."

"A lovely day, lovely day, lovely day ...," Jane whistled along with the music playing on the radio, "lovely day, lovely day..."

The phone rang.

Jane answered hesitantly, "Hello?"

"Yes, this is Mrs. Preston, Ellery Elementary School nurse. Is this Mrs. Volsandt?"

"Yes," Jane had learned that to agree with the title, Mrs. would avoid undesired lengthy conversations about a mother not being married. This pissed her off, but instead of arguing, she learned to smile and say, "Yes, this is Mrs. Volsandt." That was still her maiden name, which was okay because she and DD had the same last name. So. Peace to the unknowing.

"Your daughter, Dandelion, is sick. We think you should come and get her."

"Sick? What's wrong?" Jane asked quickly.

"She has a temperature of one hundred one and is telling me she has a bad headache," the nurse seemed very concerned, "and she vomited once since she's been in my office. She needs to go home. Give her an aspirin and put her in bed. Call your doctor if her temperature doesn't go down in a couple of hours. How soon can you be here?"

"Oh", Jane reluctantly spoke, trying to think clearly, "I can be there in an hour".

6

Then she thought about her hesitation and explained, "Oh …
I'm uh… I have to shower and dress. Oh, I'll be there as soon
as I can. Thank you for calling."

After hanging up the phone, Jane felt awkward. Why did she
hesitate? Why didn't she want to rush right down, dressed or
not, to get her poor, sick little DD?

Jane knew why. She always got frustrated when something
ruined her high. She knew she shouldn't have gotten high in
the first place and felt guilty about being caught. So, she went
against the rules she had set up for herself, allowing grass to
remain in her life after George. Losing George was too hard
without an escape. The rules Jane set for herself were only at
night when DD was asleep or if DD was at the babysitter's.
She stuck to her rules almost all the time, except when she
had a hard day or memories of George flooded her mind
relentlessly, a day like today, after a night like last night.

Twenty minutes later, Jane was at Ellery Elementary. She
went straight to the school's office and asked for DD. "My
daughter is sick; nurse Preston called me," She told the
woman at the front desk, "and I'm here to pick her up.
Dandelion."

"Oh yes, Dandelion, cute little first grader, she's been lying
in the nurse's office. I'll tell the nurse you're here." She
shuffled away quickly.

A few minutes later, nurse Preston appeared through another
door and held DD's little hand. DD fiddled with the beads
around her neck with her other hand as she walked with the
nurse.

"Mommy!" DD looked up at her mother with teary eyes. Her
cheeks were flushed bright red, and her curly blonde hair was
all messed up from lying down on the bed in the nurse's
office.

"Are you alright, baby?" Jane asked with sympathy as she squatted down and reached out for her little daughter.

"Oh, Mommy, my head hu-u-urts so bad." DD cried softly in her mother's arms as Jane gently stroked the back of her head, feeling how warm her fragile little daughter was.

"You'll feel better at home, DD. I'll give you some of your favorite popsicles. Doesn't that sound good? What color do you want?" Jane was looking hopeful at DD.

"Okay, Mommy," she held her mother's hand.

Jane thanked the nurse again and took her little girl home.

"Why did he leave me with her?" Jane cried out loudly once they got home. She always questioned Leo's leaving when times were trying with DD. "Why didn't he want me anymore? Why didn't he want our precious baby? We were in LOVE." She beat her fist on the table and growled. Jane knew, even to this day, she would still take him back. She just couldn't let go of her first love.

CHAPTER 2

Science was Jane's favorite subject in school. Her class was right after lunch. If she ever wanted to skip a class, it would never be this one. Jane was inquisitive and loved learning the weird things science had to offer. One of her classmates was very interesting to her as he seemed to know what the teacher was saying at all times with no question. He wasn't just smart, she thought; he was interesting. Something about him intrigued Jane.

"Leo, what did that experiment tell you?" The teacher asked him one day. "That I don't know shit," Leo laughed as he answered. The class roared, and Jane looked at Leo with a cocked head, like what are you doing? The teacher sent Leo out of the classroom. After school that day, Jane saw Leo walking to his car. She ran up to him and asked why he cussed in school. He told her that he thought school was a joke. "How much of that stuff do you think we are really going to use after school? I'm going to be a mechanic, and none of that stuff is being taught at this school." He was serious. "My dad taught me everything I need to know. If you have a car, you have everything you need. If you can fix someone else's car, you have a mechanic living in you. And that's what I'm doing." His smile was disastrous to Jane. The chiseled jawline, the eyes so desirous. She silently agreed with what he said. She wondered why someone like Leo even had to go to school. He was so very smart. And cute! And he had a car!

"Want a ride home?" Leo asked when Jane hadn't continued walking. "Check out my car."

"Okay," Jane blushed.

On the way home, Jane was silent. Leo talked about himself and the Vietnam war. How he hated the war, saying it was useless killing. Jane wondered about Leo as she stared at his profile. When he asked her if she wanted to go with him to a protest in the park on Saturday, Jane quickly agreed. She smiled lovingly at Leo when she got out of his car, telling him thank you.

At 8:30 on Saturday morning, Leo was at Jane's door. She was shocked to see him so early. "What time is the protest, Leo?"

"All day, Jane. I want to go early and see if I can score."

"Score what?" Jane asked.

"You know, some grass. You smoke grass?"

Jane wondered if she had gotten herself into something her mother warned her about. Mom told her to stay away from unruly boys. But Mom wasn't here. Jane couldn't even tell her Mom that she liked a boy. Mom was in heaven. Jane quickly shook her head of the death dust, trying to forget it.

"My dad does. But no, I don't, I have... Let's go."

"Leo, hey man!" A voice from the park. "Want to blow some grass, man?" The voice emerged as a tall, bearded, handsome man. He was holding a joint as he spoke. Of course, Leo said yes, and Jane followed him to a bench along the path. There, they watched as the 'tall man' lit the joint and passed it to Leo. Jane coughed hard when she took a puff and waved the smoke away from her. Still, she took another toke.

As Leo and the tall man talk, Jane admires Leo's knowledge of the war. She admired his looks and had a hard time keeping her eyes off him, his surfer blonde hair and deep blue eyes.

When the crowd started forming for the protest, Jane was surprised to feel Leo grab her arm. He looked her in the eyes and said, "I never thought I would say this to anyone, but I love you." He held her hand then and kissed her on the cheek. Jane smiled when Leo led her into the trees, still holding her

11

hand. She wanted him to kiss her on the lips. And he did. Jane was pushed up against the bark of a sycamore tree and kissed over and over. Who cared about the protest anyway. Jane wanted Leo.

In the weeks to come, Jane and Leo became the couple she had always wanted to be a part of, and she fell in love hard. She couldn't think of anything but Leo. She lay awake at night thinking of him.

She called him, and they talked on the phone about Nam, weed, and love that night. Free love. Who needs a piece of paper to make love. It's love, after all, and love is free...

On a warm spring day after school, Leo took Jane to the park, and they spread a blanket on the grass. He kissed her lips and neck and touched her breasts as he wanted more. He said it was his way of showing her how much he loved her. "It's making love," he said as he kissed her over and over again, "And I love you." Of course, she believed him. With all of his promises and soft touching, of course, she gave in.

After school was out for the summer, Jane saw less and less of Leo. Wondering why, she worried he had another girlfriend and asked him if he did. "What? You think I'm cheating on you?" was his reply as he tried to make Jane think she was nuts. This made huge worries for Jane. She knew in her heart that Leo didn't love her anymore. He didn't look at her the same way; he didn't kiss her with that hungry emotion anymore. She didn't know how to fix it. He wouldn't talk about it. And more, she didn't want to believe it.

When her period was late, later than usual for her monthly, Jane's first thought was to tell Leo. She hoped he would pay more attention to her if he thought she was pregnant. Wrong. Free love turned out to be just that. Free. Free of commitment, free of responsibility and free of marriage, even when pregnancy appeared. Leo just left. Not one word. He

12

didn't call, and she hadn't seen him in school when the fall semester began. She wondered if he was dropping out of high school like he always threatened to do. When Jane hadn't heard from Leo in over 3 weeks, she called his house.

"Oh, uh, Leo?" his mother answered as if she hardly knew the name when Jane asked for him, "Leo is at the park... I think he's protesting the war."

Jane knew right away what that meant. "Thank you, Mrs. Pinske."

Jane threw the phone into its cradle, knowing that Leo had only been involved in these protests for his own benefit. He knew he could always score grass there, always getting a good deal. Knowing there were many dealers at these scenes, Leo went every chance he got, hoping to score a whole lid or at least some of the recent good stuff coming in from Viet Nam. What a ridiculous situation, Jane thought, trying to stop the war but also wanting those spoils of war. She knew a guy who had gone to Nam and had come home safely with pounds of real stoney grass. Not the ordinary weed smoked. This stuff had big globs of sticky grass. Good stuff unlike any other she had tried. A regular smoker now, Jane enjoyed the spoils of war.

Jane sometimes went with Leo to these protests. She really did hate the stupid war! Guys dying for no reason at all. Fighting and killing people, and if they didn't die, they came home to nothing special. Just grass. No peace. No one said thank you for defending us. People looked at them as if they only got caught in a mud hole and felt sorry.

"FTW" was spray painted on everything flat, and Jane agreed with it. She wrote it herself on everything she could write on or spray paint on. Walls, fences, and the school rock where the kids went to smoke at lunch. They couldn't outright say "fuck the war" because people were afraid of the government. The cops were "pigs." They hated the freedom people had.

13

The kids who were figuring out life without parents in control. The awakening, turn on, tune in…

Leo told Jane one time about a guy who had come back from Nam and was still in shock. He had just left the place he was sitting to go jump in a small pool of water out in the field. He left his clothes where he had been sitting. He heard big blasts, and when this guy came back, his clothes were all blown to bits. It was a story of being in the right place at the right time. Other guys from Nam had similar stories. They were all scary. One friend came home without half of his arm. FTW.

CHAPTER 3

Jane lived in Alameda, a city in the bay between San Francisco and Berkeley. She liked to shop in Berkeley on Telegraph Ave for the far-out skirts and blouses she found regularly at a cute little place called Amy's, where incense burned at the counter and beads hung from the dressing room doors. She rode the bus over there at least twice a month with her friends. They all had groovy cloth and beaded purses from Amy's.

Jane journeyed to the park in San Francisco, where most of the protests were held. She was hoping to find Leo, honestly thinking maybe he would be happy to see her. The bus trip was long and made Jane feel like throwing up. The driver was nice and told her as she got off the bus to watch her step and to be careful because "all those hippies are protesting the war in Viet Nam again. Heard it was pretty wild in the park; you might want to stay away from there."

As she exited the bus, he took a second look at her in the long jean skirt, tie-dyed t-shirt and flowered hat. "Oh, well," the driver mumbled to himself, "kids these days."

Jane was never so wrong in thinking that a trip to the city would bring any good. Leo was there all right when she got to the park and having a good time with another girl. This girl had a ring on every one of her fingers, and she was hanging on Leo's neck, kissing him like she was madly in love. She practically showed her ass to all who would look at her in the shortest mini skirt Jane'd ever seen. Her long brown hair covered his shoulders. Leo seemed to be enjoying the girl and what she was doing to him.

Jane's heart began to beat wildly.

Leo turned to kiss this other girl when he spotted Jane in the park. His head quickly turned away when he saw Jane looking at him. Jane motioned him to come over. He got up, grabbed the other girl's hand and ran with her into the crowd of people chanting, "Make Love, not War!" He never once looked back.

Jane knew Leo had seen her because her eyes found his for a quick, panicky moment. Her face reddened, and she started panting as if out of breath. Her heart raced.

Her mind floated to their first time: heart beating fast, breathing heavy, sweat dripping. Leo looked at her and smiled as he held her tightly. They had just done what she had never done before. Their eyes glazed over, and they each took another swig of the wine bottle they scored earlier that day. In between kisses, he told her he loved her over and over again as they lay on the darkening cool lawn holding each other. Finishing the bottle of wine, they smoked another joint. "Such sweet love," Jane thought to herself at the time, "no one else has this love like I do. I am such a lucky girl."

But not now!

"Fuck him! Fuck him!" She said it out loud over and over again, her tears turning to anger and the anger turning into a swift run all the way to the other side of the park.

Her heart was crushed. Tears began streaming out of her eyes. She made it to the other side of the park and sat down beneath an old Sycamore tree. Sobbing, she put her head in her hands for a long time, occasionally finding enough hope to look up and see if Leo was around. He never was. Finally laying on the ground, Jane cried hard into the grassy dirt. "What a bummer," she said to herself out loud, "how could I get burned like this. Like this!" Jane screamed. Wishing for a tissue, she used the hem of her skirt instead and didn't care about the snotty dirt mess.

After what seemed to be a very long time, she got up and tried to straighten herself. Wiping her eyes with the clean part of her skirt, she noticed that dandelions were growing beside her, blowing in the soft breeze. She picked one, held it in her hand, admired its beauty and lifted it into the sky.

"Little flower of freedom," she thought into the universe, "please, little flower, be my friend and blow away all of my tears."

She puffed on it and smiled as the flower blew apart and drifted into the air. She watched until she couldn't see it anymore and thought about freedom. Being free from Leo. Could it be possible? Can her heart renew like the flowers? She picked a clover flower and sucked on its stem, tasting the bittersweetness. Then she gathered a bunch of the flowers and arranged them in a circle. She put the stem of each one into the stem of another one, and that one into the stem of another one and so on until the circle was complete. She put it on her head like a crown, and looking up to the heavens, she thought to herself, "What a pretty earth we have." And Jane was the princess of all.

Suddenly, almost like a clap of thunder, "What a beautiful problem I'm in now" flooded Jane's mind. She began crying again.

Walking slowly with her head held down toward the edge of the park, she almost ran into someone. He smiled at this cute little hippie girl as she apologized. A handsome man with dark long hair and a heavy beard. He noticed her tear-streaked face. Jane noticed a wooden cross around his neck.

"Nice cross," she complimented with her head still down.

"Thanks. Nice skirt," he returned the compliment

As she walked on, he asked her a question, "Do you know Jesus?"

She thought about it and wondered whether to answer or run. "Sure, he's someone from the Bible, right?" she felt woozy.

"He is God. If you pray to Jesus, He will save your soul from hell."

Thinking she was already in hell with the shit she was going through at the moment, she looked away. After a heavy sigh, she turned to walk away. Fighting back more tears.

He touched her shoulder, "Jesus loves you. Anytime you want to talk to him, he will be there for you. Jesus loves you. I love you too, sister." The bearded man turned his focus on her eyes and saw the tears beginning. He knew in his heart she would be all right and that his job was done.

Contemplating what she had just heard and what she felt by his touch, she continued on with her head down. Thinking she had heard this message before, she wondered who that bearded man in the park was (was it Jesus himself?) and how he was brave enough to talk to strangers about church. And if Jesus loved her, why was she going through all this pain? Figured it was because she got pregnant, cause she did a bad thing with her boyfriend. She dismissed the whole incident and wandered to the edge of the park where the bus stop was. Feeling woozy, she sat on a bench to wait for the bus. A man was standing a few feet away, making some strange noise. She saw he was bald, not completely; he had a long, skinny ponytail in the middle of the back of his head. He was wearing a long white robe. Jane eventually recognized the noise as chanting. She read about that somewhere. Slowly, she could make out the "hare Krishna, hare Krishna..." chant. He looked at her. She was tired and wished the bus would come soon. Jane really hoped he wouldn't talk to her.

But he did, "Peace, young eternal soul."

She just looked at him and smiled. She knew Papa would smile.

Jane got home after another long, sickening bus ride. She pulled the cord one stop too soon and got off the bus before she realized where she was. So, Jane had to walk past the creepy old house that she persistently stayed away from and down three more blocks. Jane slammed the front door when she finally got to her house and shut herself in her room. She cried all day, pacing her bedroom, coming out only when she had to.

CHAPTER 4

When he got home, she kept her father at a distance by telling him she was on her period and grumpy and to please leave her alone.

Jane's dad, Hank, was a hippie before his time. Grass and hash were a regular part of both her parents' lives. Her dad knew a hell's angel from work at the pier and got turned on to weed by him. After that, the friend became Hank's dealer, keeping him in good supply. Her mom went along with whatever dad did, so she started smoking it, too. Jane had the far-out folks who attracted her not-too-good friends. She was embarrassed easily in front of her good friends when dad or mom stumbled into the kitchen smelling funny, smiling, and hardly able to talk as they fumbled through the fridge.

Her friends knew Jane didn't like how her parents acted but all of them seemed to adore Jane's mom, Dee Dee. Mom was a good listener, understood the heart, and always gave the best advice, especially about boys. All the girls giggled with Dee Dee. And they knew she would keep their secrets.

Only a couple years later, Mom found out she had a brain tumor. It quietly and slowly killed her. The headaches she suffered from started making her vomit. Then she became dizzy, couldn't see well and talked incoherently. After she finally decided to see him, the doctor said it was too late to do anything for her mother. Thankfully, she died in her sleep.

Jane pushed her dad away. He was no help because now all he wanted to do was drink alcohol, something Hank didn't use to do. Before Mom died, he only smoked stuff and was mellow. Now, he wasted away every night in a bottle of whiskey.

"Dee Dee, my lady, where did you go? Come back, my lady. I love you so," is all he ever mumbled with tears in his eyes. Now, only whiskey eased his pain. Jane couldn't comfort her dad. She was in pain too and needed comfort herself. Her dad wasn't helping any.

Early one morning, as it was raining, Jane looked out her bedroom window at raindrops sliding down the glass. She considered how they were like tears. Is God crying? Does God cry? …

Jane decided that she had to become responsible. Even though she thought she was already grown up, she realized she had a long way to go. Jane started contemplating her new condition. She didn't want to become a mother, especially not all alone. She was only 15. Jane had no idea what to do or how to do it. It was three years ago, when Jane was twelve, that her mom died. She wished mom were here now to help her with this overwhelming problem she had to face all alone. Sure, Dee Dee would smoke a joint while contemplating the mess, but Jane still knew mom would think it through and talk it out with her, helping her in any way she could. Her mother loved her to no end.

Jane had always wished to have a sister or brother, thinking life would be so much better having a sibling to talk to. But she was the only child her mother would have.

Her grandma died when Jane was nine. She remembered her grandma's hugs and how she always smelled, having a "White Shoulders" scent. She always remembered her grandpa, Papa, and his after-shave scent. She had no aunts or uncles like all the other kids talked about having, and she often wondered what it would be like to have a big family. She eventually succumbed to being a loner.

And for now, the only family she had was her dad, who was either working or drunk. She inherited the household chores when her mother died, so she had to wash the dishes and the clothes, clean the house and cook. Her dad brought home the groceries and gave her the money to spend. He was a good father, providing almost everything Jane needed except "being there." He said thanks for his dinners. Not that her cooking was good, but thanks for cooking. She appreciated that much and always smiled at him for it. He never smiled back. She knew that if dinner wasn't ready, he wouldn't eat; he would only drink. So Jane knew she had to cook to keep him alive. She felt all alone right now and very afraid of her new situation.

CHAPTER 5

An older woman Jane regularly visited in her neighborhood was the closest friend she had right now. Jane met her one day at the bus stop. She and the woman talked about lots of things as they waited for the bus to take them downtown. Irma was a large black lady who wore a pretty scarf tied up on her head. She had a laugh that was loud and highly contagious. She smoked non-filtered cigarettes like a chimney and spoke with a low, raspy voice. Jane thought Irma might have sung like Janis Joplin when she was younger.

While waiting for the bus one afternoon, Irma asked Jane about her skirt. "I took my jeans, cut out the inside leg seams, and then put this material in the middle. Now it's a skirt." Jane beamed proudly at her accomplishment.

"You're so clever, girl," she said, "It's beautiful!" Irma had a way of making Jane feel special.

That day, Jane went to visit Irma.

"Whatcha gonna do, child?" she asked when Jane told Irma she was pregnant. "A girl your age, being pregnant and all. How'd that happen? No, don't tell me, I know." Irma was flustered. She lit another cigarette, then sat down and looked at her crossword puzzle. She looked at Jane again and asked, "What happened, child?" Her eyebrows were scrunched, her head tilted.

"I dunno, Irma. I love Leo, and I thought he loved me too; he told me he did all the time." Jane cried, "But Leo left me, and he already has another girlfriend! He told his friends I was a whore, Irma, and he doesn't even care that I'm pregnant with his baby."

Irma rocked her in her big arms while Jane cried softly. Irma didn't know what to tell Jane; goodness knew what to say. So Irma whispered a quick prayer, "Jesus, help me, please."

Then, with a knowing grin, "This will be YOUR baby, Jane, none of his! He don't deserve something as special as a baby. Boys like him are no good, and best to keep that kind far away." Irma spoke gruffly. "Way away from you. Way far!" She adjusted her scarf and her stance.

She patted Jane gently on the belly, "How many months are you?"

"I don't know, but I haven't had my period in a long time. I think I've missed it three times now."

"Hmm," Irma was hard-working, thinking about what to tell this poor child in need. "Now, what about school, Jane?" Irma asked, "You ain't even through high school yet! Oh, my. Oooh, myyyyy!" Irma rolled her eyes.

She grabbed Jane and gave her a big hug as she repeated her prayer, "Jesus, help me, pleeease."

Jane, being only fifteen, was very naïve. She was in wonderment about her pregnancy; a baby inside her belly was unimaginable. She really didn't comprehend the magnitude of motherhood. Thinking she was the adult in her house, she was still a child, needing so much. She wondered how she would manage all of this.

The idiots from school were insulting her, "Free LOVE and PIECE! Ha, Ha!" The rowdy friends standing by supported their spineless pals, "Oh Jane, how did you get KNOCKED UP? How does THAT happen?" Then they huddled together and laughed like children.

She was glad when the principal called her to his office that dreadful day. He told her it wasn't good for her to be there, pregnant and all, that she would disturb the other kids. Then, he courteously told her to leave school. What? She was being kicked out of school!

"Good," Jane thought to herself, "now I don't have to put up with the idiots. But what am I gonna tell dad?" Apprehension set in deeply as she walked home from school. "What am I Gonna Say? I have to tell the truth." Tears rolled down her cheek.

Jane needed her mother and again wondered why she had to die. Why her and not the drunken bastard she has left to call dad? Why not somebody else's mom? She hated herself when she thought these things. But she couldn't help it right now. What would her mother do? What would she say? She knew her mother would do something to help her. She always did. Her mom was always there for her. Always. "Mom, can you see me? Can you hear me? Oh, mommy ..." Tears flowed.

"Irma, will you help me? Please." Jane was in tears as she sat in Irma's cozy living room. She was there a lot these days. "I want to keep my baby, and I don't care about high school! I just want someone to help me out with the baby, someone who knows how to take care of babies, and you are the only one I know who can do that." Jane pleaded. Irma sighed and succumbed to the girl's disdain.

Just then, the baby kicked for the first time. Jane straightened her posture and waited to see if it happened again.

"Irma, Irma! I think the baby kicked! Here," she placed Irma's hand on her swollen belly. "Feel, it kicked again! Can you feel it, too?"

Irma held her hand where Jane told her to go for what seemed to Jane to be forever, and then Irma felt the push of a tiny foot and then another. Jane's eyes lit up as she looked at Irma,

25

"That's my baby!" Jane was elated. "That's my very own baby! Alive, inside of me!" Jane began to cry and laugh all at the same time.

Irma couldn't let her down. She had known Jane for years now. Knew all about her mother, too. She knew how Jane loved flowers in her hair and beads around her neck. Irma watched Jane transform her jeans into skirts using flowered fabric for the middle. She knew Jane's yearning for true love. Irma knew how Jane strangely loved the rain, especially walking in it, singing her very own tune, "Rain makes flowers grow, thank you rain, thank you so."

She was such a special flower child with such a free spirit. Irma couldn't help but envy her a little. But she just didn't know what to do for her now. All she could think of was to pray.

Later that night, Irma told her husband about Jane and her decision to help with the baby. "She doesn't know the work it is to raise a child," she told her husband, "Her free love is costing her."

"You don't know what this is costing YOU, Irma." Her husband scoffed at this plan. "We've raised our children. Do you really want to start over, do it all over again?" He stomped his foot as he complained.

"Won't be." Irma scolded. "She's a smart little girl. She'll learn quickly and want to be alone soon enough. I just want to help give her a good start and teach her some things. She don't have nobody else to teach her about babies and such since Dee Dee passed." Irma was determined.

"I hope for your sake you're right." Her husband walked out of the room, shaking his head.

CHAPTER 6

"Dad," Jane carefully spoke to her father.

She tried to catch him before he started drinking, so as soon as he got home from work, "I have to talk to you, Dad."

"What, Jane?"

She could tell by his voice that it was too late; he must have had one or more on the way home. "Dad, you know Leo, right?"

"Sure. Anything wrong with the young boy? He's not in trouble again, is he?" His expression was slushy.

"Well, sort of," she hesitated, "but I'm really the one in trouble, not him." She looked down at her belly.

"Jane, what? What have you done? And don't tell me you're knocked up!" His look changed to furious.

Jane was scared. She'd been around him enough times when he was mad to know his fury. But she couldn't wait any longer.

She softly replied, "Dad, I have a friend to help me with the baby…"

"The BABY?! You let Leo take advantage of you? Screw you? Shame on you, Jane! You're just a whore, just like your mother! Well, don't come crying to me, Jane, because I won't help you. Shit"   He poured himself a whiskey. "You didn't even make it to sweet 16. Guess you grew up way too soon. Damn your mother for dying! Damn it! You were HER baby. She's supposed to take care of you and all of this stuff." Sitting down, he put the whiskey to his lips and chugged it. He began to cry, just like a kid losing his mommy, "Dee Dee……………… I want my Dee Dee."

27

"Mom had nothing to do with her death. If anyone did, it was you!" Jane had never yelled at her dad that way before, and it surprised her. The tumor her mother died from was in her brain, and they thought her frequent headaches were just emotional stress. Jane blamed her dad for her mother's stress. Said he had something to do with her needing to be perfect. So, she used him for the anger that came to her after Dee Dee's death.

"And she was not a whore! And neither am I. Don't worry, Dad, I won't come to you for anything. I never do, anyway. You just don't care about me anymore! That's all. Ever since Mom died, you've been drunk. DRUNK! She was my FRIEND, Dad, and you, YOU don't even know I'm here." She stormed out of the room.

He watched her in disbelief. She never talked to him like this. "Wonder whazup with her?" The fuzzy brain returned, and he made another drink, forgetting all about what Jane had just told him. Dismissing the entire incident. He called her name and wondered where she was as he rolled a joint.

Grabbing her sweater, Jane took off. Walking fast and hard, she headed for the park where she always went when she had to blow off steam. The maintenance man was there, and one couple was sitting on a blanket in the grass, eating what looked like apples. No kids on the swings or slide. The teeter-totter was still. All in all, the park today was pretty empty.

She climbed up on the old train and sat in the engine compartment for a long time thinking, contemplating her dad's drinking, fuming, hating her dad, hating Leo even more, screaming at the world, angry with solid anger. Her soul saw heavy blackness.

The baby's kicks awakened her. Reminded her of life - a good life inside her. She better take it easy. So she quit screaming, but she couldn't stop thinking. Did her dad ever really love her mom? What about her? Did he love his daughter? Ever?

She realized her very own father wanted nothing to do with her. He was ashamed of her. This hurt. She couldn't stop hating him. Hating life. Hating what had happened to her. She felt like the victim in this situation, and her dad couldn't help her. Didn't want to. Wouldn't even listen. Jane avoided him after that day.

CHAPTER 7

"You have to go to a doctor, Jane," Irma demanded.
"You gotta do things right from the start. I think there's a doctor close enough to home so you can walk to your visits. I'll find out his name and make an appointment for you, Okay?"
Irma was hoping Jane would follow her plan. She knew it would be a start if Jane had a little responsibility. And walking to doctor appointments for Jane was a great responsibility. Being on time wasn't Jane's best trait.
Her first appointment came quickly, and she made it there on time. She wore her jean skirt with the embroidered yellow flowers (a little bigger) and pinned her hair up to look older. The doctor knew how old Jane was. When he told her she was too young to be pregnant, Jane began crying. The kind doctor put his arm around her, consoling her. "I'll help you have this baby, Jane" he assured, "and my nurses will help you too." The attending nurse kindly nodded in agreement. She had warm eyes and a soft touch as she held Jane's trembling hand. "I don't know how you will manage with a baby at your age, but I will do my best to keep you and this baby healthy." Dr. Litner said sincerely as he looked at her chart.
The nurse gave her some tissues, and Jane stopped crying. She truly believed the doctor when he said he would help her.
"I'm sorry," she said as a few stray tears rolled down her red cheeks. She dabbed at her nose.
"What's done is done," Dr. Litner gave her a squeeze as he told her, "Today is what we have to take care of now. Today is the first day of the rest of your life." Then he winked at her.

Jane looked forward to her doctor visits after this one. She liked Dr. Litner and respected what he had to say. He was very loving, unlike her own dad. Why couldn't her dad be more like Dr. Litner? He used to be; her dad used to love her and play with her. He'd tease her when she tripped, calling her clumsy-mumsy. And she really was clumsy. It was when her mom died that her dad quit being loving to her. He just disappeared into alcohol. Hardly ever spoke to her anymore. Just the necessities like what's for dinner and whether she needs anything from town.

He had difficulty looking at Jane because she reminded him so much of her mother, Dee. Her smile, her strawberry blonde hair, even the way she walked. He didn't want to put Jane off, but his heart was shattered, and he would just as soon not look at her. Not see the traces of his true love in his daughter.

Jane wished he would say hello in the morning or just smile at her occasionally. But he never did. He hardly ever looked at her.

CHAPTER 8

Jane soon began to like her pregnant body as it grew and the feeling it gave her. She felt all bubbly and full of love. Just to know she had a real live baby growing inside made her smile. Feeling the movement of its stretching arms and legs was amazing to her as she watched her belly move for long periods of time. She watched her baby roll like a wave. She wondered what it would be, a boy or girl. She visualized herself dressing a little girl in flowers and lace. A boy? Well, she'd deal with him if it were. A boy wouldn't be so bad. She imagined mud and a puppy.

So thankful for Irma and her love that Jane was over at her house most of the time. She spent the night when Irma's husband was out of town on business meetings. It was on those nights they would have fun watching TV until early morning, drinking hot herbal tea, and eating popcorn and junk like Twinkies and Ho-Ho's. Irma said she could only eat junk once in a while, and she liked it just as much as Jane did. She kept her cupboard stocked with goodies. Irma thoroughly enjoyed these nights with her young friend.

What Jane really craved was rhubarb, raw sour rhubarb. A long red stick of the stuff satisfied Jane's craving. Suck on the stick and peel it as you go eating the red flesh inside. She wondered why it wasn't pickles, she craved cause she had heard so much about pregnant women and pickles. But then she always liked pickles, and she figured this was why. Her body had already had a pickle fix. She chuckled to herself. So why crave rhubarb? She questioned herself and wondered what in her body needed. Was it sour? Was it the baby that needed it?

The monthly doctor visits turned into bi-monthly visits and then weekly as her delivery date got closer. Jane's stretched-out body was getting tired a lot lately, and she wanted the whole thing to be over with. She started walking funny, tilted backward with her belly protruding in front. It became hard to get out of Papa's chair.

"You just be patient, child." Irma told her almost every day, "That child of yours will be a handful soon enough."

Jane cried a lot. She was tired of being pregnant. She now had a hard time getting up and down the stairs. Her back ached, and she didn't like walking funny. Occasionally, she got sharp pains in her groin, which the doctor told her were ligaments stretching to accommodate her pregnancy. She wanted all of this to be over and wanted her body to be normal again, whatever that was like. She could no longer remember life without being pregnant.

CHAPTER 9

Not being in school was tough for Jane. Knowing her friends were going to junior prom without her was very upsetting, and she hated Leo even more. Her friends are in their pretty dresses with their boyfriends proudly on their side, and here she is, hardly able to wear a nightgown over her huge round belly. Alone, she was so jealous. Inside herself, she succumbed to being different. She assumed she would be alone for the rest of her life.

Jane's English teacher suggested a tutor to help her finish the school year. So, a woman came to Irma's house with all of Jane's schoolwork three days a week. This helped Jane stay focused. Every Monday and Wednesday, she had assignments. Then, every Friday, she had to take a test. Tuesdays were doctor visits, which now seemed to wear her out. She did most of her studying on Thursdays and cried if she couldn't get her homework done.

Friends from school called her a few times when their parents weren't home to catch them talking to "her." They were banned from seeing Jane.

"She's a bad influence on young girls," Karla told Jane in a gruff, manly voice imitating her dad. "My father told me that as if I was gonna do you – know – what with my boyfriend. Just because you did! He's so stupid!" Karla, the only friend she had left in school, eventually stopped calling Jane, too.

Jane cried almost every day lately and asked Irma, "Why won't this baby be born? Why do I cry so much? Why did I do it, Irma, why? No one else got caught. And almost every girl I know did it. Why me?"

"Well, child, guess I shouldn't call you child any longer, MISS Jane." Smoke bellowed above her head with the smoke rings she had just blown. Irma's eyes were full of love and knowledge as she admired Jane. She held Jane's hand and patted it lightly as she continued, "Well, Miss Janie, it's all part of bein' pregnant. It's those womanly emotions of yours. Hormones. You'll get over it., just you wait an see."

She took another drag off her shortened cigarette. "Having a baby is a big production. And that baby won't be born until it's TIME. And Your child knows when that time is, so just hush up about hurrying it along." She blew the smoke away from Jane and squished out the butt of her cigarette.

Irma was just as anxious for the baby to get here, but she didn't let on, especially not on these occasions when Jane was teary-eyed and sensitive. Irma knew the time would be any day now.

Jane's dad tried to reconcile with her but to no avail. When it came to her mother, Jane was sensitive. She couldn't forgive her dad for the things he said about her mom that day. She needed an apology from him. Her mom didn't deserve that kind of treatment. She deserved to be remembered lovingly with kind thoughts.

"Janie, honey, please talk to me. I'm your father and soon-to-be grandfather of your baby," He said, full of remorse, "I want you to know, honey, that I put some money in the bank for you. Your name is on the account, so if something happens to me, you will be able to take care of yourself and the baby." He humbly watched her for a response.

"I don't want you or your stinking money! Just leave me alone." She was angry, "Where were you when I needed you? You wait until the baby is about to be born to even try to care?

It's too late, too late for you to be 'grandpa.'" She got even angrier. "You're just the bummer drunk that lives in the house I grew up in. My mom loved me. Now, just leave me alone, you unloving soul. Go smoke another joint!"

Jane left that day with the intention of never returning home. But it didn't take her long to figure out she messed up. Even though she was angry with her dad, she shouldn't have talked to him like that. Guilt began to creep in. She was nicer than that. Her mother did teach her manners. And Papa taught her to love. Oh, Papa. She cried silently, wishing he could fix everything. Always having to "fix everything," she thought to herself, "why is everything always broken?"

"Irma," Jane asked when she crept into the kitchen back door, seeing the busy woman at the sink, "what should I do now? Now that I've ruined my dad's life as well as mine?"

Irma turned around, drying her hands on her apron. She shrugged her shoulders and scratched her head. Jane was so young and had so much yet to learn about life.

"Oh, Miss Jane, I swear, soon everything'll be just fine. That's all I can say to you now. Be patient. Your father loves you, Janie, no matter what you think, and he'll be alright. So will you. One day, you'll become family like you should be." Irma relaxed onto the wooden kitchen chair with a heavy sigh. She reached out to hold Jane's hand and said, "Just wait a little while. You'll see, I promise everything's gonna be just fine!"

CHAPTER 10

In the later part of a restless night, Jane woke up screaming. She thought she was having a nightmare when the pain hit her again. She screamed for Irma, but Irma wasn't there. Jane was at her dad's house; that's what she called it now.

"Irma, Irma" she still yelled for her. Jane relaxed a minute and then screamed again, this time much louder, a long, drawn-out scream of agony.

Her dad ran into her room. "Jane, honey, are you alright? I heard you screaming." He honestly seemed concerned.

Just then, another pain hit her. She collapsed onto her bed crying, "Go away, go away. It's my baby, and if I lose it, it's my loss."

She was shocked to hear him reply, "You're not gonna lose your baby, Jane, you're gonna HAVE it. This much I know. I was around when your mother had you, and you're acting just like she did. I think we should get you to the hospital." Her dad was serious and seemingly sober. Jane was surprised at his knowledge and wondered again if he did care after all.

Jane cried as she packed her toothbrush into the small overnight bag she had prepared at Irma's suggestion. She didn't want her dad to take her to the hospital. She didn't want him there.

"Irma was going to take me."

"Do you want to wait?" he asked, eyebrows raised.

"No, no, I can't wait. I, I'll call her."

As Irma's husband answered the phone in these wee hours, he was in a stupor, "Yeah...?" He fumbled for the light.

"Tell Irma I'm on my way to Alameda Hospital. Dad's taking me now. Ohh…" She cried again as she hung up the phone.

Irma's husband rubbed his eyes as he told his wife what he heard, "Jane's on the way to Hospital. Sounds like the baby's a comin'."

Something was wet! Wet dripping down her legs as she hurried to her dad's waiting car. As she slowly slid into the front seat of the car, she cried, "I'm all wet. What's wrong with me? Is my baby alright?"

"You're fine, Honey," her dad reassured her, "that means your water broke." He smiled to himself proudly for knowing.

"What do you mean?" she asked. "How do you know what's going on? How could you know anything?"

"The baby floats in the water bag while it's in your belly. The bag of water breaks before that little baby's born."

She remembered Dr Litner telling her something about this now, but at the time, she didn't have a clue as to what he was talking about, so she didn't pay much attention. Her interest in that particular visit was only WHEN. When would she have this baby? She didn't care How.

"Is that what hurts so bad? Dad?" She held onto his arm. "Oh, NO," She grabbed her belly and hunched over.

Another pain hit her just when they were getting out of the car in the hospital parking lot. "OWWW, UHHHH, it HUUURTS!"

She cried sporadically as they trudged into the Hospital. When they got to the admissions desk, an older woman looked at Jane in disbelief, thinking to herself, "A young hippie girl, having a baby by an old man … what IS this world coming to?"

"Yes?" she asked with questioning eyes as if there may be another reason that they were there besides the most obvious. "Can I help you?"

"My baby! My baby's coming!" Jane screamed.

The woman put her into a wheelchair immediately and motioned for one of the nurse's aides to take her to the labor room.

"I'll be there in a few minutes," her dad yelled after her.

"Oookay," her voice faded away.

The woman behind the desk looked at Jane's father, who was still in disbelief, still assuming he was the baby's father. A high-rolling sugar daddy like you read about in romance novels. She hummed silently, "Hm, hm, hm…" doing the admission paperwork.

He realized this lady may have the wrong impression and said, "I'm the girl's father. She has no husband. No mother. Long story."

"Oh, I see." replied the nurse, rolling her eyes in disbelief.

He caught on to her attitude.

"Oh, no, you DON'T SEE!" he wished for a drink.

"She's a good girl, SEE THAT? She's in pain, SEE THAT? Now I'm going to be with my daughter." He was trying to be calm, but he just couldn't think of anything except that his daughter was in pain and that she was very scared. And he needed the drink he knew he wasn't going to get.

"Wait!" The woman behind the desk commanded.

The woman quickly finished the paperwork, having Mr. Volsandt sign several pages. Then she told him where the elevator was and which floor to go to.

He climbed the stairs, not wanting to wait for the elevator. When he got to the maternity floor, he heard Jane screaming from behind a closed door.

"Damn you, Leo, DAMN YOU!" He kept repeating to himself while walking as fast as he could down the hall toward her voice.

Finding her all alone in a room near the nurse's desk, he almost came unglued when Nurse Elaine came in.

"Hello," She smiled at both of them.

"H'lo," Jane managed to smile back.

"Hi, and I'm not the baby's father! I'm the girl's father."

"Oh, I know that, Mr Volsandt, don't you fret any," the kind nurse assured, "we will take real good care of your little girl. Now, why don't you go down the hall to the waiting room? I'll call you when we finish prepping her. Okay, sir?" she sounded sincere and understanding.

"Okay, I guess; if you need me, just yell, and I'll hear you. I'll be right down the hall. She's my only daughter, you know."

He left hesitantly but a little relieved to have his daughter in the care of this nurse. He fell fast asleep on the couch in the waiting room and was awakened by Nurse Elaine about an hour later.

"Mr. Volsandt," Nurse Elaine whispered, touching his arm, "your daughter went into the delivery room a few minutes ago. I don't think this baby will wait too much longer. If you can be patient a little while, we will come and get you to see your new grandchild."

Nurse Elaine smiled as she walked out and quickly headed toward the delivery room. She was just as anxious for this baby's arrival. Jane reminded her of her own daughter. Oh, how Nurse Elaine hoped that this wouldn't happen in her family, exciting as it was.

Jane's dad was still groggy. Punching his jacket into a pillow, it didn't take long for him to fall back to sleep,

Irma threw on some clothes and rushed out the door. At the Alameda Hospital front desk, she asked for Jane Volsandt. The receptionist told her she was there and what floor she was on.

"Can I see her?"

"Go up to the maternity ward, third floor, and talk to Nurse Elaine. She's in charge." The nasty woman was exhausted and at the end of her shift. She couldn't wait to get home and tell her husband about the sugar daddy and his little baby.

Irma was near the delivery room when she saw a nurse holding a small bundle rushing out of one door and into the nursery. She knew it was Jane's baby, so she went to the nursery window and saw another nurse washing a newborn baby. As she got closer to see better, the nurse she saw carrying the baby into the nursery quickly walked out the door. Irma approached her, asking if it was Jane's baby in there. The nurse told her it was and that Jane's dad was in the waiting room, which is where she was headed. Did Irma want her to tell him she was here?

"No. I'll see him later. He needs to see his daughter right now, not me. What is it, a boy or girl?" Irma asked as she turned to leave,

"A girl."

Irma quickly left the hospital, smiling, thinking Jane and her dad may reconcile at last. And a girl, just what Jane wanted. She smiled all the way home, imagining a pink ribbon in baby hair and flowers on a sweet, puffy dress. Tears filled her eyes. Irma was so happy for her little friend. Thrilled at the prospect of helping her with the baby. She knew all would be wonderful.

"Mr. Volsandt, Mr. Volsandt," Nurse Elaine woke him up, "Come with me, Mr. Volsandt."

He got up and followed her down the hall to a room filled with flowers. Jane was asleep, so the nurse took him further down the hall to the nursery. Large glass windows overlooked all the babies. They all looked alike to him. One of the nurses saw him and went over to the newly born infant. She picked up the tiny child and brought her to where Jane's dad stood.

"She's so... so beautiful," tears rolled down his cheek.

"Precious, sweet granddaughter. She's perfect." Nurse Elaine gave him some tissues and asked him if Jane had decided on a girl's name.

"Yeah, what was it," he searched his memory, "some kind of flower; oh, what was it?" he couldn't remember.

He didn't want to admit to the distant relationship he and his daughter had. He really didn't know the name she had finally decided on. But he did know that if it was a girl, she wanted a flower name. Oh, why, he now thought, had he been so cruel to his sweet daughter?

"That's okay," said the nurse, "you get some rest so you can visit with your daughter when she wakes up. I'll let you know when she does."

"I'll be in the waiting room, thank you."

He wiped the remaining tears in his eyes as he walked down the hall. "She IS a little angel, isn't she, her mother Dee Dee, my lady?" Hank always spoke to his late wife, thinking she could hear him. He knew she was still with him; he could sense her presence, and he could still feel her love.

Nurse Elaine was checking her heart rate when Jane woke up. "Good Morning, Jane. How do you feel?" she asked.

"Fine, I guess," she rubbed her eyes and looked around. "Where's my baby?"

She checked Jane's blood pressure next.

"She's in the nursery. Such a sweet child. I'll bring her to you when she gets all prettied up. What did you name her?"

"Dandelion Daisy," Jane sleepily told her.

"Oh, how pretty. Flowers do match her little beauty." Nurse Elaine beamed. "And how did you come up with that name?"

"Thank you." Jane proudly replied. "Dandelion because they fly free prettily and Daisy because they're love flowers, you know, "he loves me - he loves me not?" She smiled, then added, "I didn't want a plain name like Jane!" And she laughed. So did Nurse Elaine.

"Beautiful Jane! You must be happy to have a little girl."

"Yeah, I didn't even pick out a name for a boy. I really wanted a girl and thought that if I had a boy, I would just name him then."

After replacing Jane's chart, Nurse Elaine went down the hall to the nursery. She wrapped the baby in a pink blanket and stared at her for a moment. Holding her gently, she brought Jane's baby to her. With a very wide smile, she handed the little bundle to Jane and watched as a little girl held a real live doll. Jane smiled at her baby and kissed the top of her head. She pulled the blanket away so she could see the whole baby. Jane counted all her tiny toes and fingers, thinking how precious they were. She looked at the bandaged place where the umbilical cord was and looked at her wrinkly arms and legs. Then she bundled her back up. Staring into her sleepy face, Jane saw her mom looking back at her.

"Mom, here she is. And she looks like you. I wish you were here with me. I miss you so much, Mom." Jane cried softly.

Nurse Elaine went back into the waiting room. "Mr. Volsandt, you will be able to visit with your daughter now. Follow me, please."

Jane looked a little washed out to him. She smiled when her dad walked in, and he was very relieved that she did.

"Hello." She was a little cool in her voice.

"Did you see the baby?" Hoping he had because she didn't want to uncover the baby again to show him. She held the baby closer to her heart.

"Yes, Jane, honey, and she's the most beautiful little girl anyone ever saw! A perfect little angel." He was elated. He touched the baby's head with his finger very gently. Jane smiled sleepily and said, "I have a baby now. I'm a mother … like my mother." Nurse Elaine came back for the baby as Jane fell back to sleep.

CHAPTER 11

Early the following morning, Irma went back to the hospital to see Jane. When she entered Jane's room, she found that the baby was bundled in soft blankets and sleeping in Jane's arms. She was smiling as Jane stared at her little new life. When Irma saw how beautiful the baby was, she let a few tears fall down her cheek.

"I'm the crybaby, Irma, remember?" Jane looked at her with love, and she understood.

"She is the most beautiful baby I ever laid eyes on, Miss Jane. The most perfectly formed angel in heaven." Irma cooed at the baby as she touched her face with the backs of her fingers. "Welcome, little one." She whispered into her soft, precious face.

"Pretty flowers, which ones are mine?" Irma asked as she looked around the hospital room, admiring the different flowers.

"They're all from you, aren't they?" Jane quizzed

"I sent some, s'pose to be in a basket."

She looked around, "there they are, those Daisies are from me." Then she looked closer at them, inspecting the arrangement, thinking she got her money's worth this time.

"So, who are the rest of the flowers from?" Jane wondered aloud. Irma looked for a card in the other flowers and couldn't find one. Jane didn't care. The flowers were pretty, and she knew they were hers.

"We get to go home tomorrow, Irma. Will you come and get me, please?" Jane begged.

"My dad's been here; he brought me here 'cause he knew he had to. Then he left and hasn't been back. He's probably at home drunk or passed out." Jane sighed and took a deep breath.

"Of course, I'll pick you up and take you home." She coughed a little into her arm. "I'd be delighted to. Anything to see this precious baby of yours. You bet I'll be here. What time can you leave?"

"They said if I could leave, I'd be out of here before noon."

"OK, I'll be here in the morning."

Irma smiled and then became very serious as she commented, "Now, Jane, tell me what you would do without your dad and your house, now, with this baby? You best be good to that man now, but don't take no bad from him neither. Uh, Hmm, You know what I mean. That will be the best way for you and him to get on." Jane wrinkled her forehead. "And if it gets too ugly for you," Irma continued, "just call me, and I'll come and get you both, any time, any day or night, ya hear me, child?" She squeezed Jane's hand and looked her in the eye. "Ya Hear Me?!"

Jane knew Irma meant every word.

Her father's house was big, an old Victorian with many bedrooms and bay windows in the living room. Jane had her own little kitchen area downstairs in what they used to call the summer kitchen. She put her bed downstairs to get away from her dad. The old cupboard cooler worked well for Jane's iced tea. The downstairs toilet was the old pull chain kind, and it was in the other part of the basement. Kinda scary, but Jane got used to it. She still went upstairs to cook for her dad and them. Irma knew to go around the side of the house where the small garden was when visiting now. The back door.

"Irma, what would I do without you? You're my guardian angel." She squeezed back on Irma's hand.

Just then, the baby burped, and they both giggled with delight. They inspected each of the baby's fingers and toes and tried to see Jane's resemblance. Irma said she had Jane's eyes. The

45

baby also had Jane's hair color; the hair she had was more like peach fuzz. Jane still thought the baby looked like her mom with her mom's eyes.

When Jane carried her new baby into her house, she smelled the nicest fragrance coming from somewhere. As she opened her downstairs door, she was surprised to see the room full of flowers. Daisies on her dresser, carnations on the windowsill, various mixed bouquets on her nightstand, flowers everywhere! All the flowers from the hospital and many more.

"Dad," she called out for him, "Dad, where are you? We're home."

She found him passed out on his bed.

"Typical, just like him. Oh, well," She was talking to Dandelion, "We can get along very well without him."

Jane knew the flowers weren't from her dad.

She called Irma. "Thank you for all the flowers. They smell so nice!"

"What flowers?" Irma asked.

"My room is full of flowers, Irma. Didn't you send them?"

"No, sorry child, your only flowers from me were in the basket, remember? Read the cards. What do the cards say? Who did they come from?" She was just as concerned as Jane was now.

She looked for a card in all the vases and found none. There were at least three dozen Daisies, bouquets of flowers everywhere, and one tall skinny vase with a long-stemmed, pure white rose in it. The words "STAR BABY" were printed in gold on a ribbon, which was tied to a sterling silver crescent moon and attached to a wire in the vase.

"No card anywhere, Irma." Jane smiled. Although she was confused, she was pleased that someone sent them. But who, she wondered. No one talks to her anymore.

46

Jane stared at her baby while she slept, thinking how precious she was. Watching her breathe, she ever so gently touched her tiny little hand, then her tiny little nose so perfectly formed. What a miracle, she thought, that a baby could bring such joy and honest love into the world. She felt a strange beat in her heart when the baby moved, hoping she would wake up, but she wouldn't dare disturb her beautiful little sleep.

In the middle of the night, when the baby cried, Jane jumped up and went to the crib. She held Dandelion while the bottle warmer heated the formula. Testing to see if it was the right temperature, she put a drop on her wrist.

"OK, little Dandelion Daisy," the name still sounded beautiful to her, "Time to eat." She sat on the edge of her bed holding the baby in her arms, and with the bottle in one hand, she poked it into her wiggling little mouth. The baby sucked for a while and fell asleep. Jane moved the bottle in the baby's mouth, and she woke up, immediately beginning to suck again.

Jane loved her little baby so much. She wondered if her own mother loved her as much. When the baby was full, she wouldn't respond to the moving bottle anymore. Jane held the baby up in her lap, holding the baby's head in her hand, and patted her back like nurse Elaine showed her to do. Soon, the baby burped, and Jane giggled with delight. "You burped, Dandelion! What a good little girl." After feeding, Jane just held Dandelion for a while, feeling her tiny heartbeat against her own. Jane wasn't tired. She was energized by all this love she was feeling. "So PRECIOUS. Mom, can you see this baby? Don't you just love her, Mom?" Jane was so happy!

CHAPTER 12

Dandelion Daisy was almost two weeks old when, early in the morning, there was a knock at Jane's door. She recognized him as someone from school. Thinking he had a homework assignment for her or something like that. The school was already out for the year.

"What?" she asked the shy-looking boy as she tried to remember his name. He had big green eyes and dark red hair, almost brown. He wore a strand of beads around his neck with a peace sign in the middle. He had on sandals.

"Oh, Jane," he replied, "I just came over to see how you and your baby are doing. I heard you had one. Is it a boy or a girl?" His eyes were darting around the house, and he was obviously looking for a baby.

"A girl." Jane was so surprised to see him in the first place, and now he seemed somehow sincerely concerned about her baby. She wondered if Leo had put him up to it. No, he didn't even care enough to hurt her. And she knew Leo was long past history now, but did he?

"Her name is Dandelion," she smiled, "Dandelion Daisy Volsandt. But I call her DD."

"What a groovy name, Jane!"

"Speaking of names, uh, yours is?"

Jane was embarrassed as she continued, "I know you, but I've been out of school for so long now that I've forgotten most of the kids in my classes."

"George". He said, "George McTocken, from the senior science club."

Well, that settled it. She instantly remembered him as the boy who knew a lot about the stars. He gave a lecture on astrology at an assembly one day. The senior science club got to do fun things, like once they got to visit an observatory. He did spark an interest in her, not for his looks but for what he knew about the sky. She just wasn't in school long enough to get to know him before being asked to leave.

"Is Dandelion sleeping?" he asked, "Can I see her? If you don't want me to, I'll understand." He hesitated, "It's just that I've been wondering about you, being pregnant and not married. I thought you wouldn't have many visitors." He shuffled his feet to turn and go.

George paused and took a deep breath, " I heard all the rumors at school, and I defended you, Jane! I know Leo, and he is a real Asshole, Capital A. And for some reason, I know you're a right-on person, and you just got hung up with the wrong guy." He caught his breath.

He continued more calmly now, "I've wanted to come over all along, but I wasn't sure if I should, being a guy."

"So why did you?" she asked, "Come over, I mean?"

"When I heard you were in the hospital, I realized how serious it is to have a baby. If you're in the hospital and all!" His eyes widened.

"I wanted to go see you there but didn't have the guts to. Now that you're home…" his voice softened. "Do you like the flowers?"

His eyes began searching the room, and he quickly continued, "Now that you're home, I thought I might be able to visit. Just see how you're doing, ya know, as a friend. I want to be your friend, Jane." He flashed her the two-finger peace sign.

Jane looked at him for a long time, not saying a word. She didn't know what to think. "Did you send all these flowers? And the ones at the hospital?" she asked, almost in shock.

"They're all in my room, and they're beautiful, George. They're just so pretty! Did YOU send them all?"

"Yes," he answered shyly. "Is that OK? I wanted you to know you had a friend. I wasn't sure if I was going to come over here, you know, with your dad and all. I like flowers too, and I just wanted to send you a smile and some beauty." He blushed a little.

"Right On. You're a nice person. Thank you, George." Jane was almost in tears and surely would have been if this had been a couple of weeks ago. Her tears seemed not to come so easy anymore since she had DD. She gave George a hug.

"Yeah, you can see DD, George; follow me."

As they walked toward Jane's bedroom, she thought about how glad she was that George had come over while her dad was at work. He'd been nice but distant since she got home. Jane noticed that her dad came downstairs to see the baby every day. He watched her with the baby a lot. She could tell he liked the baby. So, above all else, she didn't want to make her dad angry, especially not by having a boy in the house.

"Oh, she's so small." George was stunned at the sight of this newborn baby. "She's cute, Jane, she looks like you. Look, she has your eyes, blue as the sky." He looked at Jane and then at the baby and then at Jane again.

"Do you really think so, George?" Jane was already feeling like she was talking to a close friend. Funny how easy it is to talk to him, she thought.

"Yeah, I do, look." They both stared at DD for a long time, watching her sleep and giggling when she moved even a tiny bit. They were children in their wonderment.

"I don't want to wake her up now, George." She said.

"Oh no," he assured her, "don't wake her up."

"But if you want to come back later, you can." She was hoping he would. It had been such a long time since she had the company of a friend her own age. Lord, she knew she

50

needed a friend. And he was so nice. She liked him a lot. Flowers, too; what more could she ask? She couldn't wait to tell Irma.

George became a regular visitor. Even Jane's dad grew to like him. On weekends, George would take Jane and DD out to the park. They practically lived at the park, staying until nearly dark on some warmer days. They lay on their backs on an old blanket under the park's biggest sycamore tree, looking far up into the branches for birds to show the baby. Dandelion enjoyed being out in the fresh air. Her first laugh was on the train. George was holding her in his lap as they sat in the cab of the old engine. He bounced her on his knee and then poked her nose with his fingertip. She giggled.

"Jane, she's laughing, look!" He did it again, and she laughed out loud. George and Jane also laughed, which made the baby laugh even more. After as much laughing as they could get out of little DD, Jane told George, "We better take her home now; I think she's worn out. Let her take a nap, and we'll see if she'll laugh again later."

"Right On." George agreed.

Jane and George climbed back down the train with DD in a sack tied around Jane's neck and waist. She wanted the baby near her heart and saw one of these carrying sacks while window-shopping a few days ago as she and George were pushing the stroller down Park Street.

"Oh, Look!" Jane beamed while peering into the shop window.

"What?" George asked as he looked in the window with her.

"Oh, I see it, that carry sack you need for my little Star." That's what he called DD now. He said she made his heart shine like a bright star at night.

He went into the store right then and there and bought it for Jane. Took the wrapping off and gave it to her so she could wear it right then. George placed DD in the sack and finished tying it to Jane's back. He looked into Jane's eyes as Jane smiled at her little baby's face. When she turned to look at George, she felt him, something more. Ignoring it, they proudly walked home, pushing the empty stroller.

"Thanks, Georgie." Jane hugged him. "You're our best friend!"

She never takes advantage of him even though Jane knows George comes from a wealthy family. They lived in the newer houses near the beach.

Jane went with George to his house once in a while. George's mom liked Jane and DD, and she was very happy for her son. She always bought things for the baby, and Jane gratefully accepted everything. Jane brought some kind of dessert when she and DD were invited over to dinner. She loved baking, and they all loved Jane's cakes and cookies, especially George's dad.

Jane liked George more all the time, but for some reason, he became more like a family member. She did feel a certain love for him, but the kind of love you feel for a brother is a good love, a teddy bear love. Jane knew George felt the same way about her.

They shared an easy relationship, peaceful and fun, and although young, they became a family based on honest love.

"Yes, love is free," thought Jane. "But Honest love is for real."

CHAPTER 13

Irma called every morning after Jane's dad left for work. Jane would tell her all about the previous day and always had something to say about George.

"You do like him, Irma, don't you?" Jane asked her one day while they were grocery shopping. They always shopped together. Irma wanted to make sure the baby and Jane got more than what they needed to be healthy and strong, so she took Jane shopping to make sure she made the right choices.

"Yes, I like George, Jane. He's a very nice boy and does seem genuinely concerned about you and DD. I mean, he's always around."

Irma adored DD, holding out her arms for her every time they arrived. You would think DD was her very own granddaughter by the way she carried on. She was just like the grandmother Jane had wished for her baby to have. When DD had colic, Irma gave her peppermint. When Jane needed to go somewhere, Irma babysat. When Jane was worried about something or had a question, she called Irma. Jane knew she was lucky to have Irma in her and DD's lives. She would be lost without Irma.

Irma cleared her throat, "Are you sure there's nothing going on between you two?" Lighting a cigarette, Irma eyed Jane with that look.

"Irma, you only wish there was. You know we are just good friends, like brothers. Honest, Irma, if there was something going on, don't you think I would tell you? YOU, of all people, would be the first to know." Jane hugged Irma and made her smile.

They finished shopping and loaded Irma's car with groceries. On the car ride home, Irma was silently thinking when Jane asked, "Why are you so quiet today? Do you feel OK?" Irma usually talked all the way home, knowing this was the last leg of their visit. But today, she was quiet on the ride home.

"Oh, I think I might be coming down with something. Feeling a little sluggish is all. And I'm just plain cold today." Irma replied.

After dropping Jane and DD off at home, Irma said goodbye and went on her way early instead of visiting so as not to give the baby any possible germs she might have.

"Peace." Jane hailed her famous peace fingers at Irma from the back door and went on her way with DD close to her heart in the carry sack.

Irma smiled, and her heart felt warm as she got back into her car. Jane's a good girl, she thought to herself, and so very young to have a child of her own. Irma did wish there were something to tie the knot between Jane and George. She knew they were already like a family and wondered why they weren't more than just friends. She wanted to be able to rest assured that Jane and the baby would have someone to take care of them. A man to run the household. The old style thinking that only marriage would work.

In the weeks to come, Irma had no energy, her arms were sore, and her fingers kept getting numb. Later that week, she went to her doctor to see what was wrong. When the doctor told her she had heart disease, Irma sobbed right there in his office. Now she understood the pain she had been feeling and the energy loss. It all made sense to her now. "Oh my Lord," thought Irma out loud.

Prescription pills, diet, exercise, quit smoking, and she would be fine, the doctor said. But Irma worried. Heart was big. Her husband told her not to say anything to Jane as the child had problems enough of her own. Irma kept it a secret and felt more stressed because of it, which didn't make things any better. She did do what the doctor told her to do. She went for nice walks with Jane and DD in the mornings when George was at school. She tried not to eat junk food, ate more greens, and cut down on her smoking....

After telling the doctor about the changes she had made, Irma said, "That's the best I can do. Been smokin' far too many years to go cold turkey."

George was soon graduating high school. Thinking of a college, he wanted to go to Berkley. It was close, and he wouldn't have to leave Jane and DD to go away to college. Jane wished she could go too but knew she needed a high school diploma and hadn't gone back to school, probably wouldn't. She hated this but loved her little girl more than anything. Missing out on school didn't really bother her, but missing her friends made her sad. Accepting this as her fate, she loved DD even more.

Her life was now OK since George. Jane knew her baby and she would be living a good, although mediocre, life. Someone loved her, and she loved back. Peace comes in strange ways.

The next shopping day, before they went for groceries, they had ice cream at the drug store, the one with the lunch counter. It was an old little building that had lots of outdated things, including the woman who ran the counter. They loved the old ice cream sodas and only had one on warm shopping days or when Irma just HAD to have one. It had been so long (eight weeks) since Irma ate any junk food she justified the splurge. Both of them enjoyed their sodas while discussing how fast DD was growing. Six months already! She was beginning to crawl now and could sit up by herself. The carry sack had gotten too small for her a long time ago.

Irma walked Jane up to her house like she always did, helping with groceries after they shopped. Really, she only carried DD back and forth while Jane carried in the sacks. They had a glass of iced tea while Irma helped Jane put groceries away. "I'm proud of you, Miss Jane." Irma beamed as she put the bananas in the wooden fruit bowl.

"Yeh? Why?"

"You're becoming quite the little mother to DD and learnin' how to cook, too."

"Thanks, Irma." Jane beamed. "I'm trying."

After drinking her iced tea, Irma left. Squeezing DD's little hand, she kissed her. She breathed in the delicate baby smell and smiled with a deep sigh.

"I love ya both." Irma cried out after them as they disappeared behind the back screen door.

"I love you too," Irma whispered to herself, "be strong." She felt very weak that day.

She turned to go, took a few steps, and immediately dropped to the ground. Jane heard Irma cry out once and then heard a thud. She ran outside to Irma and saw her helpless body lying on the sidewalk.

"Irma, Irma! What's wrong, Irma?" She knelt down and grabbed Irma's arm, shaking it. Jane cried and began screaming for help, holding DD even closer to her heart.

Jane shook Irma's arm again. "Irma, I love you. Please wake up, Irma. IRMA!" She screamed so loud. DD was crying.

Hearing Jane scream hysterically, her dad came running outside, asking, "What's going on out here?"

"It's Irma, It's Irma! Please help her! She fell down. Hurry!"

"Go call 911 while I see what I can do." He told Jane.

Her dad ran to Irma's side and tried what he knew of CPR. Just as the ambulance arrived to take her to the hospital, Irma's husband showed up. He had tears in his eyes as he ran to his wife. The emergency operator called him and told him his wife had fallen, where she was, and that she was going to the hospital. He held on to Irma's hand as the medical team loaded her into the ambulance.

CHAPTER 14

The months following Irma's death were hard for Jane. The baby cried a lot and didn't sleep for very long at a time. Jane also cried. This brought back memories of her mother's death. Why couldn't she have a normal life with a normal mother and be a normal teenager? She felt cheated out of life. She felt alone. She had DD and now George but still felt a big emptiness inside. A huge hole came into her heart! She was angry at God and asked why. Why would God hurt her like this? Where's the love? Where's the bearded man's Jesus now? She thought he was supposed to love her.

Jane became bitter at her dad, blaming him for her loneliness and heartache. She hated him and quit talking to him. She always managed to be downstairs when he was home from work and awake. He would pass out soon enough, and then she wouldn't worry about him coming down to see DD again. She hated living this way and wondered if she would ever live like a happy person with a happy life.

She smoked weed and drank a lot of wine.

An old friend from school phoned. "Hi Jane, this is Karla. I just called to see how you're doing. It's been a while, how are you? How's your baby? Heard you had it." She was bubbly.

Jane hesitated before responding. This was the girl who was her friend once. When she got pregnant, many friends disappeared, including her best friend, Karla. And Jane knew the reason why. Karla's dad didn't want her to hang around a pregnant girl.

Jane didn't like anyone calling her daughter "it" either. She sighed and said, "Hi Karla, long time no see. She is a beautiful little girl. We're both fine." She took a sip of wine. "What's happenin'?"

"I heard you and George McTocken are together. I think that's far out! Is it serious? Are you getting married?"

"No." Jane laughed, thinking how ridiculous, "We're just good friends. In fact, he's the best friend I have now." She lit her joint again, waiting to exhale, "How are you, Karla?"

"OK, I guess." Karla had a secret and wanted to confide in Jane, thinking she was the only one who would understand.

"What do you mean 'I guess'? Is something wrong?" Jane really did care; after all, they were friends all through grade school.

"What's wrong?" She asked again.

"Oh, nothing really. I have a new boyfriend." Her voice was much happier now.

"His name is Craig, and he's a senior. He's really far out. I've been going with him for about 3 months now."

"Wow, three months, right on, Karla." Jane sensed Karla wanted to

talk more about this guy and so asked her, "Why don't you come over someday and see my baby, DD? We can catch up."

"I'd love to see your baby. I was hoping you wouldn't be mad at me

because … you know…" she hesitated, "DD? Her name is DD. What?"

"Peace, Karla," Jane didn't want Karla to feel bad. "Having a baby has made me grow up, and I understand a lot of stuff now. I'm really tuned in."

"Her name is Dandelion Daisy."

60

"Right-On. Beautiful name. Oh, Jane." Karla grinned into the phone with her eyes shut. "I'll come by this Saturday."
"OK."
"Peace, later."

Early Saturday morning, Karla showed up while Jane's dad passed out upstairs. George was helping his dad do something around their house. Jane really looked forward to this visit with her old school friend. She liked Karla.
Karla looked different. Her dark hair was really long and straight; she was wearing beads around her neck and had on a long paisley dress. She carried a cloth purse from Amy's and wore some funny-smelling perfume.
"Don't you just love my smell, Jane," Karla asked as she bounced in, "it's patchouli oil, an earth scent. Craig wears it, too. Isn't it wonderful?" Karla was happy to be there. Jane stepped back. She wondered how Karla could really like the musty stink and assumed it was because her boyfriend wore it. She said nothing about it.
Karla told Jane how the girls in their classes had changed; some were already talking about college and marriage.
"Only a few of them are hip like us. You know, all grown up and knowing about life and stuff." Karla winked at Jane.
Karla continued with her update, "And some older girls are taking pills now so they won't get pregnant. I wonder if those pills work. You know all the girls 'do it,' right? They just don't tell. Good girl fakes. Phonies."
Jane wondered about Karla's statement, thinking that Karla had gone all the way with her boyfriend, and that's what the 'knowing about life and stuff' statement was all about.
"Have you 'done it' with Craig?" Jane asked boldly.
Karla smiled as she said, "Just one time, well, maybe two or three times. Oh, Janie, yes, YES, and I like it, don't you? Holding his warm body next to mine is the grooviest feeling!

And he loves me! He tells me so all the time." She was beginning to sicken Jane.

"Just don't get burned, Karla; Leo told me he loved me all the time, too. And you see what happened to me. Is this Craig guy serious? Are you two talking about getting married?"

"No, Craig says free love is where it's at now, that nobody needs to get married anymore, it's just a piece of paper anyway." Karla took a breath and continued, "If we love each other, we will stay together, and if not, there won't be any divorce stuff to go through. He's into freedom. He wants us to drive across the states when we get out of school. He has relatives in New York." She closed her eyes and sighed.

Jane didn't say anything. She couldn't. After all, who was she to talk? And the thought of driving across the country with your boyfriend actually sounded like fun to her.

"Where's DD?" Karla finally asked.

"She's in the bedroom just now waking up. Come on, let's go see her." Jane smiled as she led Karla to DD's crib.

"Ah, Adorable, Far Out, Jane!" Karla looked at Jane, "She looks like you."

Jane wondered why everyone always had to make that comparison. It didn't matter to her, and she still thought DD looked like her own mother. Jane picked up DD and sat on the floor with her to change her diaper. Then they went into the garden, watching DD play with a doll while sitting on a quilt.

They talked for a long time, catching up on everything. The people they knew who went to war, the ones who didn't come back (there were only two they knew of), and the Viet Nam protests, where they each spray painted FTW. Love, peace and happiness. Not much about school.

Karla just loved DD, oohing and awing over her every move. Jane was a little worried when Karla wanted to hold DD but let her anyway, taking her back almost immediately when DD

62

began to cry. She was sure the smell of perfume was what made her cry, but Jane didn't say a word.

"Hey, let's go to the park with DD." Karla beamed.

"OK, it's a nice short walk. DD and I love the park."

Jane dressed DD in a pink jumpsuit with flowers on the bib and pink booties (the ones Irma knitted for her), and she put a white bonnet on her head. She put DD in the stroller, and then she put a blanket in the backpack.

Karla seemed even more excited than Jane. "Yay, let's go!" she jumped on the sidewalk.

The air was warm and sunny as they made their way to the park. Jane was happy that Karla had come over. It had been a long time since she and Karla had talked. She needed a girl talk right about now, with all the crap she had been taking from her dad and the recent death of her friend Irma. It was calming just to know Karla was with her.

When they got to the park, they put the blanket down under the same tree that Jane and George usually sat under. The biggest one had roots that grew on top of the ground, making a half circle. The park was rather quiet for a Saturday. DD fell asleep on the way, so Jane laid her down on the blanket very gently. She covered her with a small blanket even tho it was warm out. She and Karla lay down on each side of the baby, propped up on an elbow, facing each other. Jane began telling Karla about her dad and the misery she was living in, just to live downstairs now.

"I understand, Jane. My dad is no piece of cake either. He thinks Craig is too old for me. But he likes him. Figure that out!" she rolled her eyes. "Why don't you and George move in together?"

"We aren't a couple like that, Karla." Jane tried hard to assure Karla that nothing was going on between the two of them. She talked about the conversations they had regarding sex.

"He's a virgin anyway, I think. How awkward that would be. Think about it, Karla!"

"OK, OK, You don't have to be a couple," Karla replied, "just be roommates as friends. Happens all the time now. Boys share rent with girls; it's cheaper that way."

"Oh, I don't know, Karla, life seems to be so tough with a baby. If I didn't love DD so much, I would wish I didn't have her."

Jane looked down. "Especially since Irma died."

"Irma died?" Karla had known and loved Irma, too. The girls hung out at her house after school many times, eating freshly baked cookies Irma had made just for them.

"When? Why? Tell me!" Karla was shocked.

"She had a heart attack one day a few months ago. It was after one of our shopping trips. I wish I knew why, Karla, why my mother died too, but I just don't know. Maybe God is mad at me. All I know is it's so hard to smile unless I'm looking at DD. I'm really glad you came by today, Karla. You were always such a good friend. It really bummed me out when you quit calling. But I understand, your dad and all."

They lay on their backs, looking up into the tree for birds they heard but couldn't see. DD was sleeping soundly.

"Jane, you and I need to do something right now. I didn't know whether or not to tell you, but I think we both need this now."

Karla pulled out a cigarette pack from her dress pocket.

"I quit smoking when I got pregnant. I knew it wasn't good for the baby, and I really don't want to smoke any more." Jane said.

Karla opened the cigarette pack and pulled out a hand-rolled smoke. "This is grass, you know, weed. I've been smoking it for months now. It's really not bad, and it makes you smile."

"I know what grass is, Karla," Jane replied smugly.

"My parents, do you remember them?" she laughed out loud. Karla laughed, too. "Yeah, yeah, I do!"

"I didn't smoke it except once in a while with Leo, but that's all bad memories now. Yes, Karla, I smoke now. Ever since Irma died, I've been smoking every day."

"Sorry about Irma, Jane. Grass is not a drug. It's an herb. God made it. It's a natural high. I think of it as a cigarette, only a lot more relaxing." Jane agreed with Karla, "Right on, sister! Let's smoke together this time."

Karla sat up on the blanket and looked around. No one was close by. She lit the joint and inhaled a puff but didn't blow it out right away. Then she handed it to Jane. Jane took a puff and coughed. She took another smaller puff. This time, it was OK. She handed the joint back to Karla. Then Karla took another puff, and this time she coughed.

"This makes you cough 'cause it's good stuff, straight from Nam." She handed it back to Jane, who took another small puff, held it in her lungs for a few seconds like Karla had done, and then blew it out.

Jane chuckled. " I feel silly. Like I'm being a bad girl, like when I first started smoking cigarettes." Karla laughed, too, and they lay back down on the blanket with DD.

Jane admired her baby and stroked her soft hair. DD began to wake up. Jane and Karla both giggled at her cute yawn.

"Let's go walk around the park," Karla suggested as she put the smoke back into her cigarette pack.

"OK, let me get the baby ready." Jane put DD in her stroller, kissing her forehead. They left the blanket there and headed for the flower garden.

Tiny blue forget-me-nots lined the trail borders. Jane loved these the most and told George they were his flowers because they were blue and he would never forget her. One big sago palm stood in the middle, and three tall royal palms at the back of this garden. Roses, daisies, gardenias, carnations, and various other flowers filled in the rest of this beautiful garden. Jane smelled all of them and said they smelled better to her than they ever had before.

"Karla, smell this one! And this one! Wow, it's like the flowers are alive for us today." Jane had flower pollen on her nose, and Karla began laughing.

"What's wrong, Karla?"

"You look so funny! Your nose is all yellow. You better watch out. Those bees don't get you. Ha, Ha, Ha. " She laughed hard and said, "DD, look at mommy, she's a flower." DD looked at Jane and reached her tiny hand out to touch her mommy's face.

"DD is my flower...... My precious little star flower," Jane sang, "Mommy loves you …. more than all of these pretty flowers …"

Jane considered the smoke and her mental sensation. A really good feeling. Good capital G, underlined! Thinking about her relaxed state of mind, she realized her mind was in a fog, but a happy fog.

"Happy fog, happy frog," Jane laughed out loud at herself.

Karla and Jane walked slowly through the park, showing DD all the pretty flowers and birds. DD seemed to be enjoying herself, looking into the sky for the birds.

After a while, DD began to fuss, and Jane knew she was hungry. They went back to the blanket, and Jane took out the formula bottle she had brought. They sat back down as the baby drank while in Jane's arms.

"Are you thirsty?" Karla asked. "I'll go get us a coke at the snack bar. Want anything to eat?"

"Yeah, good idea, get me a coke and some cotton candy. That sounds good, and some peanuts, too. Boy, I'm hungry. Thanks."

On their walk home, Jane let Karla know that she had a good time, "I haven't had this much fun since before I left school. Thanks, Karla, for turning me on to that grass." She giggled. "I thought you would like it, I do. Relaxing, huh!" Karla smiled and pinched DD's cheeks, making her smile too.

"No wonder my dad smokes even tho he drinks. And my mom, she had the best life." Jane thought back to when her mom was alive, and now she was sure that her mom had benefited from this smoke.

"When will we get to meet Craig?" Jane asked when they got back to the house.

Karla thought about it and then said, "Let's get together when George and you can go out with us somewhere. Do you ever get a babysitter? We can go someplace righteous and have a groovy time."

"Yeah, George's mom babysits for me once in a while so George and I can go somewhere. Where would we go?"

"I'm not sure, maybe a concert, Hendricks or Janis, but you'll have fun, I promise you that."

"OK, Karla, I'll call you when we can go. I'll talk to George."

"Right on, Jane!" Karla beamed.

"I better go home now. I'm happy that I came over. We always did have a fun time together, but today was extra special." Karla gave Jane a big hug.

"It really was good seeing you again. I'm so glad you called Karla. Keep in touch. Later." They hugged again and then waved the peace sign as Karla walked away. Jane smiled again, almost laughing all the way up the sidewalk to the back door, thinking of the good time she had had that day.

CHAPTER 15

George came over later that day, and Jane couldn't wait to tell him about her day with Karla, but she let him finish talking about his day first, how his dad taught him all about the plumbing in a bathroom. The proper way to remove and replace faucets in a sink and replace shower heads using this white tape junk. George was impressed with everything and enjoyed spending time with his dad.

When he was through telling Jane about his day, and she had listened closely, she then told him that Karla had come over, "Do you know her?"

"Yes, I do." He answered, "She's nice, I guess. Did you have fun?"

"Oh yeah, and we went to the park with DD. She's all worn out and sleeping now." She hasn't told George about the grass yet, but she would do it at a better time.

"Karla has a boyfriend, and she wants us to go out together and meet him." Her voice became excited as she continued, "Do you think your mother will babysit for us so we can go out with them some night? Do you want to go, George? I think it would be a blast."

"Sure, Jane, when do they want to go out?" he liked going out with Jane. He liked pretending all to himself that she was his girlfriend. He really wanted her to be, but in trying to be the friend she said she needed, he dared not take it too far.

"I told her I would call when we could go." She smiled.

"OK. I'll talk to my mom." He went in to see his little star and asked how DD liked the park today. Jane told him DD discovered the flowers and just smiled. "She laughed a lot too!"

George and Jane went outside in the backyard when it got dark, bundling DD up like a mummy even though it wasn't cold. George put down a blanket and told Jane to lie down on her back. He laid beside her with the baby between them and said, "Look up, Jane. See the stars? They shine for us, and one of them is for DD all alone." George smiled at Jane as he watched her stare into the sky.

"Which one, Georgie?" Jane asked without looking at him.

"Whichever one shines brightest."

They searched the sky for the brightest star, and George pointed out the constellations that he knew. "Ursa Major is where the big dipper is. And there's the little dipper." As they lay there, George desperately wanted to grab Jane's hand and kiss her, but he didn't. He knew Jane respected him for respecting her. He would do nothing to jeopardize their relationship. He valued Jane highly.

Later that night, Jane thought about what Karla had said about moving in with George. How nice that would be if it were only possible. How could she do this? Jane wanted to say something to George about it, see what he thought. She was grown up with her own baby now and needed to be free. She wanted to raise the baby in a loving environment, thinking being with George all the time would be the best thing for DD.

The next afternoon, when George got to Jane's house, he smelled weed. He asked her if she smoked it, and when she told him yes, he almost fell over backward! "Why didn't you tell me?" He asked, laughing. "I don't care. Lots of kids do. I tried it once but didn't like it. I got paranoid."

"Oh George, you didn't tell me…". Jane got out a cigar box. "Now, since DD's asleep, let's smoke." She smiled widely.

"Uh, No thanks, Jane. Not my thing." George quit laughing now. He put his chin in his hand and contemplated this.

Jane offered him a glass of wine. "It's strawberry wine, my favorite." George said, "OK, I can handle that. Sounds good."

They drank the wine, the whole bottle. "Good, huh, George!" "Right On, Janie!" They didn't know strawberry wine was low in alcohol.

When DD cried, George went to her crib. "My little star, do you want me to pick you up? Huh, DD?" She looked at him lovingly as he held her. He was wondering if she could smell his strawberry breath as he carried her into the backyard where Jane was. She grinned at DD and thought to herself, "Yes, this is right."

"I want to be the grown-up I've become. On my own." She told George boldly the next day. "What do you think about moving in with me? DD would love it, George. And I would cook for you and do laundry and the housey things that a mother does." Jane took a deep breath and continued, "What do you think, George? It would be good for DD." Another deep breath, "I just have to be free. You know, like the flowers and the stars, if only for a short while. I want to bloom Georgie, OR." She shuffled her feet and rocked the stroller DD was sleeping in. "We can go to Berkeley and find one of those communes or join some Jesus people. They're nice."

"Don't talk like that, Jane. Where's your head? Of course, I'll move in with you." Trying to hide his excitement, he spoke calmly, "I'm sure mom wouldn't mind. She loves you and little star. A commune wouldn't be good for DD." He stepped closer to Jane and took DD out of her arms.

Jane began to worry that she was asking the impossible, even though George was eighteen. Maybe his mom wouldn't let him move out of their house and in with her. She shuddered and began contemplating being alone forever. Maybe Karla could move in with her.

"OK, we'll move in together." George interrupted her thoughts.

Jane couldn't believe her ears. He really will do it. Tears filled her eyes, and then she got excited. Her heart beat faster. The tears ran down her cheeks. "Are you sure?" she asked George again. "There is no better friend than you in the whole world, Georgie. I'm a lucky girl." Jane leaned over and kissed George on the forehead like she often did when she couldn't contain herself. Then, Jane gave him a bear hug. "Thank you. Thank you, George. What will your mom say?" George rolled his eyes.

A couple of days later, George called Jane with the good news. He talked to his dad and his mom. They consented to this arrangement. "Wow, George, I didn't know your folks were so nice." Jane beamed.

"Yeah, they can be. They both talked about it and agreed it would be best for DD." George responded. "He told me that he expected me to be a responsible man and that he wouldn't allow this if he thought I wasn't. And then he warned me that I'd better be or else!"

"When can we do it?" Jane was anxious but paused a moment before saying, "Oh, by the way, my dad was upset at my wanting to let you move in. A real bad scene the other night." She lowered her head.

"What'd he say?" George asked. His shoulders slumped, and he sighed heavily.

"He said no way… at first." Jane lifted her head as she continued, "But I told him it was happenin' one way or the other, and he couldn't stop me. He screamed at me, and I yelled back. I told him if he ever wanted a relationship with his granddaughter, he had better let me, or else I would stay away from him downstairs for the rest of his life until he died." She continued, "He cried, Georgie." She sighed. Then she looked George in the eyes, "But then he said he only wanted what was best for DD and me. He said he loved us. And he actually hugged me! Then he said as long as it was you, George, you could move in, and he would even help us if I wanted him to." Jane jumped for joy!

"Groovy, Jane." He jumped with her, holding her hands.

Jane remembered the days, "You know, my dad used to be the best ever! He always took me places when he wasn't working at the piers, and sometimes, he took me to the piers with him. He told me how longshoremen were 'bosses' and that I was a 'boss daughter.' It made me feel special. He used to love me. I guess now he still might… a little."

George gave her a quick hug and said, "Let's go to the park." Then he held his arms out for DD. He put her in the stroller, bundling her up with a blanket and her cuddly teddy bear.

They walked to the park. DD wiggled and cooed as they walked. Jane looked at George, who was also looking at her, and they laughed just out of sheer joy.

"Star Man?" Jane questioned him, "Or Uncle? How about Uncle George?" They discussed the name DD would be calling George.

"Call me what you will, Jane and my little star will call me what she wants." He beamed and gently stroked the back of DD's fuzzy little head. She had hair, but it was thin, and you could hardly see it. 'Stardust flower fuzz,' George called it.

"George, I'm so happy you came into my life. Did I ever say thanks?" Jane was bouncing the baby on her hip near the swings.

"I love you, Jane," George told her that often, and she knew it was only the brotherly love he spoke of. Although sometimes …

"We love you too, Georgie." Jane kissed his cheek. He pushed Jane and the baby in the swing.

They skipped halfway home, laughing with DD. At home in her crib, DD lay down right away. "She's tired out from the park," Jane commented as they both watched her fall asleep. Jane got the cigar box and began rolling a joint. "Hey, Jane!" He watched her as she rolled it. "Perfect." George wasn't mad or unhappy. He was impressed that she could roll a good joint, though.

She lit the candle on her table. The one stuck in the old wine bottle. She lit the joint and blew out the first puff toward George. "At least get contact with me." Jane laughed.

George breathed in like he was getting all the smoke and began to laugh. Jane handed him the joint and said, "Here, have a toke." She smiled when he took it. He took a puff and began coughing. "Small tokes, Georgie!" He took another tiny puff and handed the joint back to Jane. "I don't feel nothin' Jane."

Jane smiled inside herself, thinking he would in a second. "Come on, George, let's go outside to the garden. Here's a coke." She handed him one of the two she got out of the old ice box.

"Don't think I can get up right now." George was smiling.

"Sure you can, Georgie! You're just hi." He looked at her and realized she was right. "Wow, I never felt like this before, Jane." They both began to laugh. George grabbed Jane's hand, and they walked together out to the yard, where they sat on a bench overlooking some roses. "Beautiful roses, Jane! I've never seen such beautiful ones!" He tried to pick one, but the stem was hard. Jane got some clippers out of the basement and said, "Try these." He clipped the rose he wanted and gave it to Jane. "Roses are no way prettier than you, Jane. But I love them the same!"

From then on, George smoked with Jane. He knew he could never roll like Jane, so he bought a pipe at the groovy T-shirt store.

CHAPTER 16

She kept DD in the playpen with her stuffed animals while she put sheets on the crib. The baby cried. Jane knew she was hungry and probably tired. She got a bottle of milk out of the old antique ice box with the motor on top. It had been there since her Grammy. She heated the milk in a bottle warmer Irma had bought for her. Modern inventions, she thought, how wonderful.

When the baby fell asleep in Jane's arms, she carefully lifted her into the freshly made crib and covered her with a fancy pink blanket. She stood there watching DD sleep for a few minutes as she often did. My baby, she thought, and now a loving non-dad too. Jane felt blessed.

She looked up with her eyes closed and claimed, "You do love me!"

George came over right after work to move more of his things and help Jane. His dad brought him in the truck with his bed and a couch. Jane had put an easy chair that she got from her Papa down there already, so now they had a hip living room. George also had his own bed, which Jane had put on the other side of the basement near the pull-chain toilet and laundry room. The basement still looked pretty empty, but they felt rich. They were now officially roommates.

So now Jane felt complete. She got a fresh look at her life and didn't seem to be so frustrated. She felt safe with George. Loved. She knew he would never hurt her, and now she even wished that she could love him 'that way.' She tried to envision it a couple of times, and this only made her laugh at herself, thinking, 'Oh, brother.'

DD loved George. Every time she saw George, she laughed and clapped her hands. When she learned to sit up, he had taught her how to play patty cake, clapping her hands together for her. George was the best delight DD had. He loved her as if she were his own daughter. He wished she were and thought often about it.

Jane and George had a good time grocery shopping and putting all their food away for the first time. All the dishes they had were oddball plates and a few cups. Pots, pans, and silverware, all from the thrift store, made the kitchen complete. The built-in cupboard was very useful. George loved Jane's cooking, saying he usually ate out at home or had dinner delivered. His mom didn't cook very often. What a treat when he found out Jane's cooking was so delicious.

Jane felt like she and George were kids playing house sometimes. But she knew it was real. Far out, a real trip.

Karla came over less often now since George was there full-time. She loved George and enjoyed his company but really wanted them to become a real couple. One afternoon in Jane's backyard, while looking at the garden, Karla said, "Jane, I miss you."

"I can dig it. I miss you too, Karla." She got up and got the cigar box. "This is some good green bud from Nam." She pinched it between her fingers and smiled at the stickiness. Karla held out her hand to feel it and then, as she smelled it, said, "What are you waiting for? Let's smoke!" Jane rolled the joint because Karla always had a hump in the middle of hers, and it usually fell apart after lighting.

"Oh, how tasty, Jane…". After this, Karla took a toke and then two.

"Yeah, sister, right on." Jane reached for it and told Karla, "Don't Bogart that joint!!" They both laughed.

Life became routine, with George going to work on weekdays. On weekends, they walked to the park with DD in the new stroller George bought. Jane couldn't believe how fast the baby was growing. She would be walking soon. She was already crawling all over the place and pulling herself up on things.

George's mom loved the little baby and wished now that George and Jane would get serious about each other. Get married. She called herself Grandma already, anyway.

Before summer was over, Jane planned a little vacation for them, just an overnight trip to the beach nearby, a camping trip. George loved being outside at night, especially when he could see the stars and the big sky. Jane did, too, and looked forward to this fun adventure. They planned it around the time of the new moon when the sky was dark and the stars were at their brightest. Jane wanted to invite Karla and some friends of George's. A real family outing. She couldn't wait and began making a list of things she needed.

CHAPTER 17

The phone rang late one night while they watched TV. Jane looked quizzically at George.

"Hello…" George went over to the phone, answering curiously.

"Hi, this is Karla. Is Jane around?"

"Janie, it's for you." She got up and grabbed the phone.

"Oh, Hi Karla, what's happenin'?" Jane was curious. No one usually called this late at night. And she hadn't heard from Karla since the night they all went out to a movie. When she and George met Karla's boyfriend, Craig, Jane thought he was OK, a little demanding.

"Please come over. I need your help." Karla cried out.

"Right now?" Jane quizzed.

"If you can, will George watch DD for an hour or so?" Karla was challenging. And very insistent.

"Sure, but what's wrong, Karla?" Jane asked again.

"I'll tell you when you get here. Please hurry." She hung up. Jane convinced George she would be OK. Karla still lived with her parents, only four blocks away…and she would call him if she needed him.

Jane left in a hurry, walking fast, down one block, then over two, then down one more before she could see Karla's house in the distance. Everything seemed to be OK.

Karla answered the door before Jane got there. She had been watching out the window, waiting. Karla grabbed her hand and practically dragged Jane into her bedroom.

"What's wrong, Karla? Why are you crying? Is it something you did? Or is it Craig?" She asked.

Jane knew Craig wasn't all that much in love with Karla. When she met him, because of the way Craig looked at her, Jane felt nervous. And Craig just didn't seem that into Karla. "Yes, he ... he ..." Karla sobbed, rubbing her eyes. They were swollen and red. "He went out with another girl! And now she's pregnant with Craig's baby!"

"What?! Are you sure?" Jane asked, "How did you find out?"

"Yes, I'm sure. Craig just now called and told me," She blotted her nose with the tissue Jane handed her, "he told me about her and said he had to break up with me because she is pregnant. I can't handle it, Jane. What do I do? I just can't handle this!" Walking in circles, Karla cried harder.

"Pregnant? Broke up! Well, that shit-faced asshole! What a burn." Jane hugged Karla tightly and knew she would have to help her through this. "Karla, what a Bummer! He must have been cheating all along, ya think?" Jane was mad and cried with Karla. "Asshole!"

Then Jane asked her, "Who is the girl, the bitch?"

"I don't know, someone from another school, a sophomore, I think. Some slut." Her anger showed. "A new pregnant whore! He said he loved me! He lied to me. He's a big fat liar." She sobbed hysterically. "I loved him, Jane, and he didn't even care!"

"Karla, don't cry. It won't do you any good. I know. I've cried, too, over an asshole just as bad, maybe worse than Craig. It only gave me a headache and bloodshot eyes. Nothing would bring him back, and you know what?" She paused ... "I don't even care anymore. That's the trick. Tell yourself you don't want him anymore and pray that your love for him will go away... and it will. That's what I did." Jane squeezed her hand, "Oh, Karla, I'm so sorry for you. What can I do to help?"

Jane hugged Karla again, letting her cry on her shoulder and telling her everything would be all right. She knew all too well how this kind of hurting felt.

"It will be OK, Karla, honest." Jane was sincere.

On her walk back home, Jane thought about what she had told Karla. Her love for Leo didn't really go away; she didn't think it ever would, but she really was over him. What else could she tell her friend, though? Jane felt Karla's pain. She knew what 'Free Love' was all about. Free. Free from commitment. Free from responsibility. Free to do as you please with any other free spirit. Free from true love!

The next day, Jane called Karla to check on her.

"How ya' doin', Karla?" She asked

"Oh, OK, I guess. But I didn't sleep at all last night. I hate him, Jane. I just hate him. How could he do this to me? Thank God he didn't get ME knocked up. ……. Oh, I'm sorry, Jane, I didn't mean anything by that."

"It's hard, I know. Just hang in there and make those boots go walking.'" Jane tried to make Karla smile, which she did for a second.

The next few days, when Jane checked on Karla, she heard the same response from her, "I didn't sleep at all last night. I was up all night pacing my bedroom. I tried to sleep, but every time I laid down, his face appeared." Karla cried a lot. Jane prayed for her.

One morning, about a week later, when Jane called, to her surprise, Karla sounded different, a little happier.

"Well, sounds like you finally got a good night's sleep. How ya doin' Karla?" she asked expectantly.

" I feel better. I slept really well. I found some of my mother's pills. She takes them once in a while when she can't sleep. I remembered this and went into her bathroom and found a bottle that said, 'Take when needed for sleep.' They're red. So I took one."

Jane was concerned, "You better be careful, Karla. You never know what pills can do."

"Yeah, I know, but they made me sleep and feel so good. It's out of sight. Have you ever taken pills or acid or anything, Jane?"

"No, and I don't plan on it. Please be careful, Karla."

When Jane hung up the phone, George was playing with his little Star on the living room floor. She liked that about George. He played with DD all the time. She wanted DD to have a man's love and positive male contact. If only George was less boyish. He wasn't very manly to her. She thought about her dad and wondered how he was doing. Then, she discussed Karla with George. "George, Karla is better now, but she took some pills, and I'm worried about her."

"What kind of pills?"

"I don't know, some kind of red sleeping pills. "

" REDS?" George was loud in his reply. "Those are prescription drugs. Where did she score them?"

"From her mother. She took them from her mother's bathroom cabinet. Her mother doesn't know. She said they made her sleep and that they made her feel good. Does that sound right?" She looked at him, touching his arm. "Is it like the stinky grass we smoke sometimes, the good Nam shit?"

"No, different, stronger. I know because I tried one once at a party at my friend's house. His mother has them, too. Yeah, they do make you feel good, but I think they're dangerous, ya know. "

"YOU took one? Why, George? "

"Just to party, Jane, my friends were taking them, and they were alright; they were just drunk. So I tried one. Nothing bad, really, and they do make you feel good. In fact,

I'm glad Karla took one. Maybe now she'll forget about that jerk and leave you alone."

Jane was confused. She didn't know George had taken pills. She thought she knew everything about him. She was disappointed. And a little curious. She wondered how they might feel if it was anything like the grass they smoked. She liked the feeling the grass gave her, peaceful fun. Oh well, she supposed it was OK since Karla felt better.

She called her again later that day. "Karla, are you sure you're alright? I'm worried about you."

"Yes, I'm fine, and I think Craig can just have his slutty little girlfriend. How much will he love her when she's pregnant fat?!" she shouted. "I'm glad he didn't get ME pregnant." Karla squeezed her eyes shut again. "Sorry, Jane." Calming some, Karla said, "I'll get over him. I know that now. But when, Jane, when?"

"I don't know, maybe when you find someone else?" Jane suggested a night out with her and George.

"Yeh, right. But who else is there?" Karla asked. "You have the only guy worth having, and you aren't even his girlfriend! Can I have HIM, Jane? That would be a groovy kind of love." Karla laughed.

Jane thought for a minute and then just said, "I'm glad you feel better, Karla. I'll call ya tomorrow."

She hung up the phone and contemplated how she would feel if Karla dated George. She couldn't stop him from dating and wondered why he wasn't dating now anyway. She knew they had something special, but she also believed in their individual freedom. If he wanted to go out with Karla, she wouldn't stop him, but she wasn't going to encourage him or even suggest it to him. Damn.

81

CHAPTER 18

When school was out in the summertime, parties happened nearly every night, either at someone's house or at the beach. That night, George figured it'd be fun to cruise by some of these parties and have a good time with Jane. He arranged it with his mom to keep DD.

When he told Jane about his plans, she hugged him and laughed, saying, "It's been a long time since I've seen lots of these people. Do you think they'll know who I am?"

"Sure, you're Jane, queen of motherhood. They will be impressed by you, too." He squeezed her hand.

"Impressed?" She didn't understand him.

"Yes, you have a baby." George smiled. "No one else does."

She pondered his statement and considered not going at all. Remembering the friends who stopped calling after she got kicked out of school, she wondered if they would still ignore her. But she knew George wanted her to go. He wanted to do this for her.

Jane dressed in blue bellbottoms with a big burgundy flower that she had embroidered on the bottom of one leg. She wore a flower print tie over an eyelet white blouse. A floppy denim hat that she sewed a blue daisy onto held the long hair out of her face. George liked her far-out style. He wore a Nehru jacket with his jeans and a string of beads, as always, around his neck. His dark red hair was getting long, almost past his shoulders. Jane admired his new looks and sometimes thought about 'things.'

"So, where to first, Georgie?"

"Brad's house, his Mom and Dad are there, but they're hip. They gave him a pipe for graduation."

"You're joking, right?" She couldn't believe that. No old people that she knew of except her parents and a few of their friends ever smoked grass.

"Sure thing, Janie, I think they smoke it too but no one knows, none of Brad's friends anyway. But I think they do, smelled it on them before." He looked her in the eyes and winked.

"Well, I guess that's okay. It's a great herb. Everyone should smoke it." Jane laughed, and George joined her.

"Right on, brother!" Jane was really ready for this party.

Brad met them at the door when they arrived and showed them the food his mom had made for the party. They both grabbed a handful of nuts, and Brad took them to his room, a cave of sorts with black lights and posters on the walls.

Incense was burning a sweet smell of strawberries. Candles were burning. Iron Butterfly's 'In-A-Gadda-Da-Vida' was playing loudly on the stereo. Jane recognized kids from school sitting around on the floor, some on the bed, smoking. It took a while for Jane's eyes to adjust, and when they did, she saw the most beautiful poster of a guy and a girl embracing in a meadow full of flowers. The flowers were shining a neon yellow due to the black light. The words 'Love is Free' were glowing in bright red. Someone passed a joint to George.

"Does Jane smoke?" Cindy asked George.

"Sure." George replied, "Well, I haven't seen her at school since she got knocked up. It's been so long that I wasn't sure she even existed anymore. Ha, Ha." Cindy laughed as she watched Jane take a toke off the bomber joint Brad had rolled and then start coughing.

"George, I don't dig her," Jane whispered to George after she quit coughing, "she was one of the girls that made fun of me when I got pregnant. Seeing her here bums me out."

"What a drag, sister." George grabbed her hand. "We won't stay here long, Janie. There are more places to go to. Groove on everything and everyone else, okay? I promise we'll leave in a flash."

"Okay." And she passed the joint back to George after she took another toke.

She was beginning to feel its effects and mellowed out a lot. She forgot about Cindy and went farther into Brad's room to see who else was there. He had a long hallway leading to his bathroom, and at the end of the hall was a door that led outside. Opening the door, Jane began to venture out, and she turned around quickly, walking fast back down the hall. Grabbing George by the arm, she told him she had spotted Leo. George immediately thanked Brad for the high and told him they were leaving. While she waited outside for George, she saw Carol, who wanted to know all about the baby. "Dandelion Daisy is the grooviest name I've ever heard, Jane." Carol sang the name, "Dan-de-lion-Dai-sie," and smiled. Jane enjoyed telling her about DD and secretly hoped it would get back to Leo at the party.

They walked to the bus stop and got on the 91, which took them across town to the north side. Patricia was throwing a happening at her house. She really knew how to make a party psychedelic. George heard she was handing out LSD. However, Patricia wasn't in the balloon-filled living room when they got there. Roy greeted them and led them down the black-lit stairs to a den where the party was really going on.

Then Roy whispered to them, "Want a joint? I got some, here."

Jane began to say no when George said," Sure, far-out man. Thanks." And he took the joint.

Jane looked at George and told him she couldn't smoke anymore. He told her he was going to save it for later, "Stash ."Then he winked at her as he put it in his shirt pocket.

"WOAH, you do think ahead." They began laughing and looked around for who all was there.

"Wonder where Patricia is?" Jane said curiously.

"Probably with her boyfriend. What's his name?"

"Eric, I think. Don't know why her mom lets her hangout with him. He's so much older, been out of school for 3 years."

"I am too, now … out of school," George laughed. "Far out!"

"This guy has a job, so I guess they think he's responsible enough to hang out with their daughter. I wonder where she or they are." They both kept looking around.

Just then, a tall guy with a beard and long black hair walked up to them and said, "What's HA A PPIN', Man?" He sounded like he'd had a few tokes along with a couple of bottles of wine.

"Hey, Andrew! What's happenin'?" George reached out his hand.

"Who's your babe, Man?" He was cross-eyed.

George looked at Jane and said calmly, "He is a friend from shop class," assuring her he was cool, "He's far out."

"She's my tight buddy, Jane. Jane, this is Andrew. We took shop together, he's a righteous artist with steel, wood or anything."

"Peace, man." Jane thought he was hip-looking.

"What sign are you?" She asked.

He handed them a pipe. "Pisces."

"Made this one myself. Try it out." The pipe was made out of soapstone and had a peace sign carved on both sides, with marijuana leaves curling around the stem.

"That's a BITCHIN pipe!" Jane grinned.

"Right-On!" George agreed. "I can dig it."

Jane was feeling very laid back, more relaxed than she'd been in a very long time. She looked around for a place to sit. No chairs were in sight, so Jane sat right where she was leaning up against a wall and slid down the wall until she hit the floor, where she pulled her knees up to her chest and held them with her arms. Someone walked by and handed her a jug of wine. She took a swig and handed it back to whoever it was. George sat down beside her, putting his arm around her shoulder. He leaned into her and asked if she was mellow. She assured George she was high and enjoying the trip. Her head swung back and forth to the music. Janis Joplin was singing ...

Andrew passed them a small wooden box and said, "Here, load the pipe again and smoke some of this. Can you dig it?" "Yeah, get it on!" George took the box and reloaded Andrew's pipe. He lit the pipe with a wooden match, which he lit with a flick of his thumbnail. He took a big hit and handed it back to Andrew, who looked at Jane. He took another toke and then handed it to her.

"No thanks, man." Jane put her head back and hummed, "I'm really loaded and just want to trip for a while." Hendricks was wailing on his guitar!

"Right-on. I can dig it." Andrew walked away with his pipe saying, "Peace everyone."

After they were at Patricia's party for a couple of hours, Jane whispered in George's ear, "Hey, man, you want to split this place and get some fresh night air? Patricia obviously isn't going to be here."

"Right On." George took her hand and led her to the front door.

They walked the long way to the bus stop. George was wishing for the car he knew his dad was going to give him in a couple of months. He had to work for his dad to pay for it and only had two more months to go. It was a 56 Chevy and currently parked in his dad's garage. It ran but needed some bodywork, which George had been working on. And tires. It was powder blue. George worked hard for it. His dad thought he would take better care of it if he actually earned the car. George and Jane enjoyed walking and talking. The warm night air smelled of flowers, and Jane was mesmerized by their fragrance, stopping at every flower she could touch. Reaching for it and smelling it deeply. "Ummmmmm…"

"Georgie, isn't the night air so beautiful … it's refreshing." Breathing deeply, she swung her arms lightly at her sides as she walked.

"Let's go to David's party," George suggested. "They're having it in the rec center at their church. I know a church! It's close by."

"Karla told me church people smoke grass, too," Jane responded.

George laughed, "This isn't like an ordinary church. They're hip to it. They're more like Jesus freaks. Lots of love and peace. David says he gets his weed from one of the girls there." George watched for a reaction from Jane.

"What a trip." She said, "Well, it's not a drug. It's a relaxing herb, and God made the herbs. Let's go to church!"

She grabbed George's hand, and they walked a little further until they got to the street where the church was. Following the voices of people talking, they located the rec. center where they found little of what they had imagined.

People were dressed in their Sunday best dresses and suits. Old people stood by the buffet to serve food. Children were running around screaming.

David was busy talking to some people and didn't notice them walk in. George and Jane's eyes darted all around the room for someone else they knew.

"Hi! Glad you could make it." A voice from behind. David had noticed them after all. "Welcome to our house of worship where we party for the Lord."

David thought of himself as being tuned in, not the LSD way but in a spiritual knowledge sort of way. Intellectually tuned in.

"Peace." Jane managed to say.

"Hi, David. What's happenin'?" George was sincere but wished now they'd left before David saw them.

"We were on our way home from Patricia's house and thought we would stop by just to say hi," Jane spoke up quickly.

"I'm pretty tired and I have to get the baby, you know." Jane told David as she looked at George who quickly gave her a nod of appreciation.

"Well, come and meet some brothers and sisters before you leave." David held out his hand.

Jane turned as she said, "Bummer ... can't do that. I have to get my baby, and I'm already late. Later, David."

"Peace, man. Later." George agreed as he followed Jane out the door.

"Jesus bless you both," David called out to them as they left. When they got outside, they both sighed heavily. Then they laughed. They ran away from the center and then stopped and laughed some more, looking each other in the eyes, singing the Animal's song, 'We gotta get outa this place if it's the last thing we ever do...'

"You know I believe in God and all that." Jane told George as they stumbled down the sidewalk, the sweet wine from Patricia's party still having its affect on them.

"So do I, but I don't like the church scene," George replied.

"Jesus loves us. I know that much." Jane whispered, thinking of the bearded man in the park.

"Those Jesus People are nice too. I rapped with a lady one day at the park. " Jane smiled, remembering. "She was real nice, and she prayed for Dandelion Daisy. That sure was righteous. She didn't seem freaky at all." Jane remembered that day peacefully.

They each had silent thoughts on their walk toward somewhere they hadn't decided on yet. "So, where to now?" George asked Jane.

"Home. I'm tired and could really dig sitting down somewhere other than the floor. Let's go crash at home." Jane smiled at him, "And besides, we have that 'stash,' remember?"

"Oh, yeah … Far out," George said, feeling for the joint in his shirt pocket. "Right On!"

"Time to mellow out with my hippest flower buddy." His smile was happy. George was glad that Jane wanted to go home.

"Yeah, and no absolutely lovable little precious baby to worry about." Jane closed her eyes as she returned George's smile. Time away from DD was refreshing sometimes, and this was nice. Jane felt relaxed and free.

They walked the rest of the way back to their downstairs abode, stopping along the way to get some munchies at the corner store.

Jane dropped into her old chair, stretching her arms and legs straight out in front of her. George took the bag from the store, got a bottle of Coke out, and filled two glasses with ice cubes from the freezer. He handed Jane her glass, put a Bob Dylan record on the stereo, and sat down on the couch. They looked at each other and sighed heavily, and then they both laughed out loud, saying how much fun they had.

"How about that, Brad? I think it was the best party. What do you think, Jane?"

"Noooo," Jane slurred, "I think the REC center is where it's at!" They both laughed hard, holding their stomachs.

Jane got up and put some nuts in a bowl, then added raisins and some M&Ms. She took it back to her chair, ate some, and then handed George the bowl. "So, Georgie," she winked, "get your 'stash'."

He ate some of the mix, and with his mouth almost full, he answered, "Uh, let's save that." he finished swallowing and then explained, "I got some reds from a guy at Brad's party. We can just crash if they're too heavy; we're home … no baby. You said you wanted to try them. Can you dig it?" Jane wondered if she could.

George got the baggie out of his pocket and, gave Jane one of the red pills and popped two into his own mouth. They drank their Coke and listened to Bob Dylan, passing the bowl full of snacks back and forth.

' … and she breaks like a little girl…' George and Jane began singing along, loving Dylan and his music.

Eventually, Jane said, " I can feel it, George; I'm very loaded." She slurred her words.

"I can feel it too," George replied happily, "what a trip.

"Go ahead and crash if you feel like you have to, Janie." George was sincere, feeling the drug taking control of his own body.

"No, don't wanna miss this high." Jane smiled and scooted down in her chair almost slipping to the floor.

"Wow, I haven't been this mellow since, ever! Mellow yellow, HA, HA! They should have called it mellow red. How's you, Georgie?"

He laughed and then stumbled to an upright position standing up, then he held his hand out to Jane and said, "Let's dance." She slipped all the way to the floor and just started laughing. "No, Georgie, I can't even stand up. Ha, Ha …"

He got on the floor and laughed with her, holding her hands in his. Then he kissed her on the cheek like he always does.

She looked at him sideways and smiled, and then he kissed her again, this time more passionately, on the lips. She liked this feeling; she was spinning in her head, and then he kissed her again. She kissed him back, and her body began to quiver. Then she laid her head back on the edge of her chair … Spinning … feeling.

Before she lost all control, she comprehended who was kissing her. She wanted this good feeling to go on, but she was confused. She stared at George for a couple of minutes and then kissed him again. Over and over. They were on top of each other before Jane realized what was happening. She knew she had always wanted this, so she gave in to the urges, letting it happen.

"Georgie, I love you…" she promised when it was over.

Right now, her brain was so fuzzy she couldn't think straight, but Jane didn't worry. She just lay down beside George with her head on his chest next to the old chair and listened to Dylan, humming along with her eyes closed.

In two minutes, George crashed on the floor, snoring loudly.

CHAPTER 19

The camping trip was this weekend. George bought sleeping bags for himself and Jane. He found a little baby bundling that would work for DD. He thought she would probably sleep with her mother but bought it anyway. He couldn't resist anything for his little star.

Jane was putting together a list:

-Hot dogs
-Buns
-Chips
-Cookies
-Sodas
-Bouncy baby seat
-Diapers & a hat
-Blankets
-Milk.

Some other people were going too. Everyone loved going to the beach. Some wouldn't spend the night but would go just to party. Beach parties in Alameda were fun. South Shore had a really long stretch of beach, connecting to Washington Park at one end. The park had the biggest portion of shore, so they went there. From there, they could walk up the tall stone steps into the park.

The beach was warm, and the ocean was refreshing. Jane breathed in the stimulating salty air as she gazed at the cool water in front of her. She carried DD down to the water, holding her tightly in her arms. When Jane stepped into the water, DD cried at first. She was scared of the lapping waves. Jane strolled in up to her waist, holding DD close to her.

George dove under the water and came up close to the baby, laughing, splashing, and getting them wet. DD giggled and, with eyes so wide, began to look around at the water curiously.

Jane squatted down to let DD feel the water on her belly. DD giggled again and splashed the water with one hand. When Jane got DD's chest wet, she squealed with delight! Hanging tightly onto her mommy's neck, DD went up and down into the water, giggling the whole time.

After playing in the ocean for a while, George took the baby from Jane and ran up to the blanket on the beach, where he sat her down. Then he watched DD crawl toward Jane as she was coming in from the water. Jane picked her up and carried DD back to the blanket, brushing the sand off of her. DD saw the sand on her little hands and tried to eat it.

Jane wiped her hands off, telling her, "Not food, sand, no eating." DD looked at her little hands curiously.

Jane enjoyed this wonderful day on the beach. DD took a nap on the blanket under the umbrella while George and her fixed their place to camp, getting the sleeping bags spread out and preparing a place for the food.

George built a fire pit out of some river rocks he found from another old burned-out fire. He gathered up some old driftwood and some dried weeds. Then George lit the fire. It was getting chilly, and the sun would set soon. He cuddled with Jane and DD, wrapping a blanket around all of them. Together, they watched the fire develop.

People began showing up: Brad and Cathy, Roy, Lee, and Cindy. Patricia and Toni came with Andrew.

When she saw Patricia, Jane asked, "Where were you at your party?"

"Having my own little private party with Eric ... if you know what I mean. Ha, Ha." Patricia was already loaded.

"So, what's happenin' with Eric? And where is he now?" Jane asked curiously.

"He's right on!" Patricia took another swig off the bottle of strawberry wine she carried before continuing, "He blows my mind when we're together!"

"But where is he now?"

"At work. He works, ya know. Can you dig it? To take care of me, he says." Patricia smiled and rolled her eyes, trying hard to keep them focused.

"Hey Andrew," Patricia blurted out, "get over here and bring your pipe. I want to show Jane."

"I saw his pipe at the party, Patricia. It's bitchin'. You got anything to put in it?" Jane wanted to mellow out.

"Andrew, load it." Patricia was demanding since she was the one to score the lid. They passed the pipe around, and when George came over, Andrew loaded the pipe again.

"Righteous, get it on, man!" George was ready to party.

As it began to get dark, everyone gathered around George's fire. Jane cooked hot dogs over the fire, giving DD her very own stick, a long one, and showed her how to hold it in the fire. But DD didn't want to hold it. She just wanted to eat, so George gave Jane a bun, and she fixed a hot dog for the baby. DD sat in her bouncy seat and played with the hot dog, pinching it into pieces and eating some of it, keeping herself and Jane entertained for quite a long while.

George walked around the camp, saying hi to everyone. Some people were rolling out sleeping bags, and others huddled around the fire. Lee had a portable radio, and 'Lucy in the Sky with Diamonds' was playing. The Beatles weren't his favorite group, but George liked a few of their songs. This was one of them, so he hung out until the song was over.

"Hey, Jane, George!" Karla yelled from across the sand.

Karla wasn't sure if she would go camping with everyone or not, so Jane was surprised when she saw her. But she was glad

94

because that meant Karla wasn't sad anymore. Jane had enough of Karla's tears the past few weeks.

"Hey, Karla, what's happenin?" Jane stood up to greet her.

"Wow, bitchin fire! I got marshmallows. Want some?" Karla handed the bag to Jane.

"I also got some other candy … not the baby kind…" Karla looked at George, smiling. George returned the smile and winked at her.

Jane took a marshmallow and put it on a stick, showing DD how to hold it in the fire as it browned. DD grabbed it, but Jane held it high and out of her reach. After it cooled, she handed the marshmallow to DD, who instantly mushed it into her face. Then she looked at her hands and began eating at her fingers. Everyone laughed, which made DD giggle even more. Then she looked at Jane and put her hands on her head as she often does when she laughs. Jane laughed with DD. The sticky mess could be cleaned easily enough, and Jane wasn't worried. She was happy for DD to get all this attention. "What a great trip," Jane thought to herself, " a baby and my best friend, a party on the beach. What more can I ask for?"

Jane got out a baggie of weed and a small tray, handing it to George. He pinched the weed into tiny pieces. Never having an easy time rolling, he got two papers and stuck them together, making a longer run at it and then began rolling the joint. It had a big camel hump in the middle where Jane held it when she lit it. She took a hit and passed it around the fire. George laid down on the sleeping bag with DD and studied the stars. He pointed out the ones he knew by name. She pointed too, and DD eventually fell asleep by George's side under his arm. So Jane took DD to her own sleeping bag and laid her down just inside the top.

Karla was impressed with George's knowledge of the stars. She scooted closer to him, watching the look on Jane's face the whole time. Jane was mellow and watching her baby sleep, so she didn't notice when Karla handed George a red. He took it and asked if she had any to sell.

"I got a bag. Part of a bag. Want a bag or just a few?" Karla impressed herself.

"Just a few for now, but when we get home, I think I'll buy a bag. These are good." George knew Jane would get mad at this, so he talked quietly to Karla.

And then Karla asked loudly if anyone wanted a red.

Jane said, "No thanks." and looked at George as if to ask if he wanted one. She knew he might.

Andrew said, "Right ON. I'll take two."

George took another one, knowing all he had to do was crash where he was. Karla kissed George on the lips when she gave it to him. She didn't care what Jane thought anymore.

George looked at Karla, contemplating this kiss, and said, "I'm tripping, are you? What's happenin'?"

The next morning, when Jane woke up, George wasn't in his sleeping bag. She looked all around for him. There were a lot of bags spread out, and most people had their faces covered.

She decided not to worry. She relit the fire, which was still smoldering, and gave DD a bottle. She lit the end of a joint and enjoyed the sunrise with her baby.

In a while, as the sun was getting warmer, she saw George get out of Karla's sleeping bag. Jane's heart skipped a beat. She tripped on this for a minute, and then she told herself she wasn't worried. She got to keep him. Just as they were, she wished peace to everyone.

When they got home after camping, Jane unpacked, put the baby down for a nap, and talked to George. He told her all about Karla and apologized for not coming to the sleeping bag. He said they got really stoned on reds and fell asleep. He swore nothing happened. "I don't even dig her that way."

Then Jane laughed, "Free Love, Man."

Jane took a deep breath and then said, "The only thing I don't really like are those reds. Karla has been taking a lot of them lately. Please be careful, Georgie."

"You know I will, Janie. Here, do you want some?" He was proud as he showed her the ones he scored from Karla.

"No, I don't like them. They remind me of being drunk, just no booze. That kind of drunk is too heavy for me. I'd rather drink wine or smoke, thanks."

CHAPTER 20

Working regularly for his dad now, George got the car and took real good care of it, washing it weekly. He loved this car. He took Jane and DD out to dinner in the car occasionally. They went to Mel's drive-in diner. Hamburgers just seemed to taste better if you ate them in the car. And DD enjoyed the ride.

George arranged DD's first birthday. Flowers were in their house everywhere. He bought the cake at a great bakery in Oakland, over by the lake. The cake, of course, had flowers all over it, with one big star sticking right out of the top. The flowers were edible, as George knew DD would want to eat them, and he wanted her to. The star would be Jane's keepsake, which was made of silver, and the name Dandelion Daisy was engraved on it with her birthdate. Karla was there, and some other friends came over to enjoy the day with them. George bought DD a big wheel to ride on. "She can hardly walk yet, George." Jane laughed at the present. Smiling, she knew how much George loved her little girl. And she loved George as much as ever. He was her strength and soul companion. And now her true love!

One beautiful winter day, George bought Jane some carnations at the florist and brought them home to her. He wanted Jane to know how much he loved her.

"For you, Janie." He smiled as he handed her the flowers.

"Far out, Georgie, they're beautiful." She nearly cried as she smelled them, burying her face far into the bouquet.

Then George handed her a beaded necklace he made just for her. It was very pretty, with violet and scarlet crystal beads on a sterling silver chain. A clear crystal heart hung in the middle. He put it around her neck and then kissed her.

"I want you to know, Jane, I will always love you and that DD will always be my little star." He kissed her again.

George was sincere as he hugged Jane, "We will always be family. The wonderful free family we are now, like no other."

"I love you, George."

"I love you, Jane."

Jane and DD came home from shopping one winter afternoon and saw George's car in the driveway. Jane was excited to see that he was home and wanted to tell him what she had bought for DD's upcoming second birthday. DD helped her pick out some things for the party. Of course, plastic flowers and hearts. Hats with flowers!

When she got in the house, she saw George on the couch and said, "Hi, Georgie." And then she went to put DD down for the nap she had already been trying to take.

"George, I'm home." She spoke softly as she walked into the living room.

"George, are you asleep?" She was worried now that he had taken too many reds and passed out. He did that once before, and she really got on his case for it when she woke him up. She was planning her attack on him this time when she got to him.

She yelled, "George, wake up. Wake up, George. Come on, George, don't scare me like this."

She was shaking him and began slapping his face.

"WAKE UP!" He wasn't moving. Jane began to cry.

"Oh, my GOD!" Adrenalin rushed throughout her body.

She heard DD crying in the background but ran to the phone and dialed 911, telling them her brother had passed out and where they were. Then she grabbed DD and went back to George. He was pale and cold. Jane didn't know what to do. She cried with the baby as she paced the room, looking at George, hoping he would wake up.

She called his mom while she waited for the ambulance to arrive. She thought his mom might straighten him out or at least put some sense into his skull about his pill-taking. That is, if this hospital scare doesn't fix him first. He knows being in the hospital is serious, so maybe this incident will straighten him out. Jane sure hoped so.

Then Jane called her dad at work.

"Please come and get DD. I have to go to the hospital with George." Giving no explanation to him. Dad agreed and willingly left work to pick up the baby.

She knew George and Karla partied a lot together, and Jane worried about how much. Several times, she checked on George when he got home from a day with Karla and found him to be so loaded he could hardly walk.

She tried to tell him he was taking too much, but he told her, "Don't tell me what to do, please, Jane, just let it be."

He was nice about it, so Jane left him alone after that, figuring he knew how she felt. After all, it was a free world.

When the doctor came into the ER waiting room, he told George's mom and dad that he had tried all he could but couldn't save George. Then the doctor said he was so sorry. George's mother collapsed. His dad looked at Jane and shook his head as he grabbed his wife. Jane was shocked. She couldn't believe it. "George!" "Georgie, NO!"

Jane ran out of the hospital screaming. She ran all the way home. Right now, her dad seemed to be the only one she wanted to be with, as well as DD, her baby, her precious little girl.

100

When she got home, she frantically told him that George died and ran into his arms like she hadn't done since she was a little girl. She cried hard into his chest as he patted her back.

"Oh, Jane, I'm so sorry." That is all Hank could muster up to say to his poor, grieving daughter.

"What happened?" he finally asked Jane when her sobs lessened.

"Pills. Those Fucking red pills." She never swore in front of her dad, but the truth is the truth, and she knew it. "I hate pills! Fuck it all!"

She wiped her nose on her sleeve and then began the long, treacherous story of what had just happened. He sympathized deeply with his crying daughter, thinking of his own wife's death.

After she gave her dad all the details in between sobs, he told her, "I'm sorry. I do understand, Janie, and I love you."

He continued, using her cuss words, "It's fucked up to lose someone you love, I know. I lost your mother." He had tears rolling down his cheeks then. She went to him, put her arms around his neck, and cried softly with him.

"Where's DD?" she asked her dad when she remembered.

"She's taking a nap. It took her a while to settle down when I got her here. She knew you were upset, and she cried a lot. But she finally went to sleep with her dolly." He was proud of himself.

"How do you live without Mom? How can I go on without George?" Jane cried, realizing that her dad understood.

"Well, you know what?" He smiled, "I know what will get you through today."

"Nothing can help this!" She screamed, thinking he might offer her some weed.

"But you need to calm down right now!" he was stern with her.

Hank went to the cabinet where he kept his whiskey. He got out two shot glasses and gave Jane one of them. He poured a shot for himself and then a shot for his daughter.

"Drink this all at once. Down it." He demanded as he handed her the small glass.

She did as he told her and drank it all at once. Then she shook her whole body in distaste. She opened her mouth to blow out the fire and looked at her dad.

"What IS that stuff?" She asked in delight as she began to feel the warming effect it had on her.

"That's what I call relief." He laughed as he poured another shot for each of them.

Jane felt the relief in her neck muscles and wanted a second shot of whiskey. She was being comforted by her dad, HER DAD! She loved him at this moment and watched him lovingly pour more relief for both of them.

CHAPTER 21

She hated Karla for the first few days and blamed her for George's death. But when Jane saw Karla crying at the funeral, she understood. She put her arms around her friend, realizing Karla also loved George. The hate faded and was replaced with sincere sympathy.

Days passed as Karla and Jane kept in touch. They were good for each other since they shared the love of one guy who was righteous. Now, they were sharing the awful grief, which made them grow closer.

Karla never took Reds again. She knew now it was dangerous and would never forgive herself for getting George hooked on them.

" He had his own mind, Karla. It's a free world. George is a Free Spirit." Jane kept reminding her, even though she needed to be reminded herself.

George was Jane's life, her best friend, and her 'family'. What was she going to do now? How could she live without Georgie? Why, Lord God, WHY? Why George?

"He is truly a Free Spirit now, Jane." Karla saw her remorse. "You know he is around us," Karla assured her, "and in our hearts."

"Yeah, but he's NOT HERE! I can't hug him." Jane sobbed again, this time on Karla's shoulder.

"He is, he's in your heart, and that's where he'll stay forever, right Jane? Right? Do you hear me?" Karla shook Jane by the arm.

"Right on. I hear you." Jane sighed heavily as she reached for George's pipe and loaded it with some of her stash.

"Here, this one's for you, Georgie."
She took a puff and passed it to Karla. Then, she touched her heart and held her hand there for a while, just feeling it beat.

CHAPTER 22

Jane's dad was nice to her, nicer than he'd ever been before. He gave her money to spend and paid attention to DD, calling her his Grand-Dandelion. He still drinks, but not as often. And when he did drink, he stayed upstairs so he wouldn't act foolish in front of DD. Just a little thing, but anything from him helped Jane.

Now realizing the loss her dad must have felt after losing his wife, his true love, her mother, Jane became sympathetic with him. Oh, how Jane has been so much wiser since George. Wiser and lonely. Life lessons she wished she didn't learn. She considered her poor dad.

Jane got a job at a nearby restaurant where she didn't need a high school diploma. There, she worked as a waitress. The people liked her, and she got good tips. The walk there and back energized her.

Her dad actually began to babysit on weekends. He came into the restaurant once in a while, with DD walking by his side and holding his hand. Jane always wished she had a camera when she saw them coming because they were so cute walking together.

Jane thought of Irma a lot and wondered if Irma could see the progress with her and her dad. She knew Irma would say, 'I told ya so.'

Karla was in her senior year and didn't see Jane and DD as much these days. She was busy with homework and school activities.

A guy from her business class took Karla out one night, and she didn't quite know what to think about him.

"He's a Church boy, Jane! If Kevin knew about my past, he'd hate me." She told Jane the next day after her date. Karla was worried about the secret she'd been keeping from Jane and fretted over anyone finding out. Kevin, being religious, made her feel like she had to confess and be totally honest with him and with Jane.

"No, he wouldn't hate you, Karla." Jane answered, "Besides, are you going to tell about your drug use? Do you have to?"

"No, but I just don't know about him. His honesty and niceness blow me away. Guess he's okay to talk to; we could be friends like you and George were... Oh, bummer, sorry, Jane." Karla winced and then quickly said, "Just don't know if I can do him." She blinked back tears.

"George lives in my heart now, remember Karla? Nothing you or anyone can say or do will change that." Jane smiled and touched her heart, breathing deeply.

CHAPTER 23

Dandelion went to nursery school when she was 4 years old. Jane walked her to school every day, even on rainy days. DD's little umbrella had pink flowers all over it; Jane's was a big clear bubble. On really bad stormy days, Jane's dad drove her even though school was only about five blocks away from the house.

One day, while she was walking to school to pick up DD, Jane spotted a house that was for rent. It was a small house with a fence around it. The sign in the window just went up that very day. It had a porch and a tree in the front yard. Jane wasn't sure what kind of tree it was, maybe an apple? She went into the yard and peered through the windows. Thought it was cute and hoped a little but didn't think she could afford it. Dreaming, she imagined how she would decorate.

After picking up DD from school, she walked back by the house for rent. She pointed it out to DD and asked her if she wanted to live there.

Surprisingly, DD said, "Yes, Mommy, I can play in the fence." Jane smiled, knowing what DD meant. At her dad's house, there was no fence, and Jane had to give DD strict borders to play in. Sometimes, when DD got carried away playing and went out of the borders, she got in trouble and couldn't go outside for a while. At this house, she could play outside without thinking about silly borders.

When they got home, Jane called the phone number that was on the rent sign and spoke to a lady on the other end.

".... I have a little girl, and this is closer to her school.... Can we look inside?" Jane politely asked.

"The rent is $250 a month. Can you afford that?" The lady asked in a grumbly voice.

"I think so. I have a good job." She was glad to hear the rent wasn't the 400 dollars she had been expecting.

"Okay, I'll show you the house. Meet me there in an hour." The lady seemed a little gruff, as if it was bothersome to her. Jane calculated her income from the restaurant, and with this rent expense, she knew it would be difficult to do. She'd have to rely on big tips, maybe take home a little extra bread. Jane went back there an hour later as the lady requested.

Jane loved the inside of the house. It had a big kitchen with windows on two sides. She would have to clean up two small bedrooms, a bathroom, and a small living room. The backyard was a dirt pile, like someone tried to fix it and quit. But the kitchen sold her.

The lady told Jane she would rent to her because of little girl, "She's an angel if I ever saw one."

Jane smiled and wanted to laugh but didn't. Not until the landlady left. Then she looked at DD and giggled, "My angel, Dandelion, you got us this house! Thank you, sweet star."

Jane told her dad about the rental that night, and he was upset, "What's wrong with this house? It's our house."

"I want to be the adult I am on my own." She was stern. "I'm almost 20 years old now. I work and can pay the rent. DD likes it too."

"Is that so, DD?" He looked at DD as she were coloring on a big tablet. She was trying to draw a house with a fence around it.

"Do you want to move into that other house?" He looked at her curiously.

"Yeah, Grampa, it's over there," and she pointed toward school. Her eyes lit up, and she went to the window to see if she could see the house. Her dad looked at Jane and shook his head as if to tell her he knew she would do what she wanted to do anyway. He was sad.

Jane arranged the new house with the stuff she had accumulated. Of course, her grandpa's old chair … she loved that chair. She only had two kitchen chairs, and since this was her favorite and fit into the kitchen easier than in the living room, she put it at the kitchen table. The living room had a couple of beanbag chairs and a loveseat. That was enough. She hung an old tie-dyed sheet in her bedroom window because the only curtain she had was in DD's room. The living room had curtains, and the kitchen could do without them because Jane liked looking out the windows. One window faced the front yard, where she could see DD outside playing, and the other window faced the ugly backyard. Jane sat in her chair contemplating backyard designs, thinking someday she might fix it up.

DD ran herself ragged in the front yard, coming in only to go potty. She had her doll carriage outside with all her dolls in it. Telling each one about their new house. "… And we have our own bedroom …" Her cute little voice squeaked as she pointed to her window.

The house was closer to school, and Grampa could still babysit. His house was only two blocks away, so DD and Grampa had lots of nice walks together. Jane enjoyed being close to her dad now, even though she was happy to be out of his house.

"Hurray for Freedom! Peace to all who visit me here." Jane was elated as she continued arranging her stuff.

She met the neighbor woman, Martha, right away. An older lady, she was the mother of two grown girls. Jane and Martha had herbal tea together on some mornings when she got back from walking DD to school.   Martha enjoyed her company and would stall Jane as she went through her front gate, "Hi, want some tea? Nice day, isn't it." Once in a while, Martha walks to school with Jane to pick up DD. She loved having a young miss around again. And Jane adored Martha.

Jane really felt grown up now, not like how she had felt while living with George. She felt grown up then, too, but not in the same way. She was on her own now, really on her own. She made all of her decisions and was responsible for her life and the life of her daughter.

CHAPTER 24

"I'm going to take your temperature. You feel warm." Jane found the thermometer when she got DD home from school. She took her temperature and found it to be 100 degrees. "Not too bad," she thought hopefully.

She gave DD a red popsicle out of the freezer and sat her in one of the beanbag chairs. Jane turned on the television to see a channel that had cartoons, hoping DD would soon feel better. Jane sat next to her on the floor, touching DD's hair and her warm little cheeks. DD began whimpering, "Mommy, my head hurts."

Jane immediately got to her knees and looked into DD's eyes, contemplating what to do next. Then DD began throwing up. Jane took her into the bathroom and let her finish throwing up in the sink. She cleaned her up and put a cool washcloth on her forehead. Sitting down on the bed, Jane kissed the top of Dandelion's head.

Then she called the doctor's office.

"Tell Dr. Litner that DD is in a lot of pain, her head hurts, and she's throwing up." The nurse told her to wait a minute while she told the doctor. When she came back on the phone, she told Jane to bring DD in right away.

Jane's dad drove them and had her there in record time.

Jane explained everything to Dr. Litner, asking him what could be wrong. He said tests had to be done in order to know for sure and told her to take DD to the hospital lab with the paperwork he handed her. There were three forms, all paper clipped together with the doctor's signature on them all. He handed Jane a few pills in a bottle for DD and said to give her one now. And one this evening after dinner. It was Tylenol. He will call Jane with the results as soon as he gets them.

On the way to the hospital with her dad in the car, Jane began rapidly asking him questions about her mother.

"Mom had headaches too. Did that have anything to do with her tumor? Do you think DD could have the same thing wrong as Mom? Does something like this run in the family? Oh, I hope not." She held DD tighter, trying not to cry as they drove.

In the hospital, they quickly found the lab where DD had to go for the tests. Scared little DD screamed during the blood draw.

"Dandelion Daisy, what a precious name." The technician that was preparing the test for her commented.

"Yes," Jane replied, "She's my little flower. My little Starflower." She looked to the sky as tears filled her eyes. Oh, how she wished for George right now. Right now, she needed him so badly.

"This test won't take long, Mrs. Volsandt," the technician knew Jane was worrying. "Soon you can take your precious little one home."

"And when will we know the results of these tests?" Jane asked.

"Your doctor will contact you with the results after a specialist looks at them," he told her. "Usually takes about three to five days. Hang in there, Mrs. Volsandt."

Jane flipped him the peace sign and sighed.

The rest of that day and the next days were the hardest for Jane. "Why? Why, why?" The thoughts going through her mind made her crazy. And "Why don't I have George to help me now?"

Anxiety and depression set in quickly. Jane prayed to God, asking Him why, and then humbly pleaded for DD to be all right. She was mad at God and told Him she got the bad end of life because He had let her mother die, and then her 'other mother,' AND THEN her best friend in the whole world. "WHY GOD??"

"And now my daughter, God? It's not fair!" She could only anticipate the worst. She paced. She cussed. She checked on DD every other minute and felt her forehead.

She called Karla and asked her to stop by after work.

"What's happening, Jane?" Karla asked, very concerned.

"DD…" is all Jane could say at first through her sobs. "DD… She's sick. I'll tell you when you get here, Karla."

Karla left work early and went to Jane's house. She found DD asleep on the beanbag chair and wondered where Jane was. Just as she was beginning to worry, Jane walked in, saying she had been in the bathroom washing her face.

"What a bummer, you look awful, Janie. What's happenin'?" Karla followed Jane into the kitchen.

"DD's sick, she's sick bad, and I can't handle it."

"What kind of sick?" Karla asked.

"I don't know yet," Jane answered, "Test results aren't back yet. Maybe tomorrow or the next day before we find out."

"Then why are you so upset," Karla asked, patting Jane's hand, "if you don't even know what's wrong yet?"

"It's like my mother! She has the same symptoms as my mom had before she DIED." Jane became hysterical.

"Jane!" Karla yelled to get her attention.

"Jane, it's not the same. It's not the same as Dee Dee."

Jane glared at Karla, "You don't know anything, Karla. What if this runs in the family? How do you know, you ain't no doctor, Karla." Jane grew angry now and repeated loudly, "How do you know?"

"I don't know!" Karla yelled back.

Karla was mad as she explained, "I was just trying to give you some peace about the whole thing. It won't do you any good to worry the whole time until you find out the results, now will it, Jane? It won't do DD any good to see her mommy crying."

Karla was right, and Jane knew it, "Okay, you're right, Karla, but what do I do while I wait?"

"Crash a lot. I got sleeping pills if you want one. I take them once in a while when I can't sleep. Sleep will pass the time away, and it will do you some good. Take one now. I'll stay with DD." Karla dug into her purse for the pills.

Jane was shocked when she heard this. She shook her head in disbelief. Karla quit taking pills when George died, didn't she?

"Karla, you quit pills!" Jane exclaimed.

"I quit Reds, that's for sure, but I still need to sleep. I can't quit taking these once in a while," Karla was adamant, "especially since George died." She began crying. "They're legal, Jane. The doctor gave them to me."

"Wait a minute, Karla. What are you telling me?"

Jane wondered what she was talking about. She thought they had both passed the sleepless nights phase since George. They went through all the phases together after George died: hate, anger, despair, sleepless nights, etc.

"Karla, why are you still taking pills?" Jane was serious.

"George," Was all Karla could say as she sobbed louder, "George."

"Karla!" Jane demanded her attention and grabbed her by the arm, shaking her. "Karla!"

"George, George, it's all my fault," Karla continued in between sobs, "George, I killed George!"

Karla was hysterical now and shaking all over. Jane grabbed her and held on tightly. "What are you talking about, Karla? You didn't kill George; he OD'd remember." Jane rocked Karla in her arms as she spoke.

"Because of me......." Karla sobbed harder now, repeating, "He died because of me! Because of me!"

Jane didn't know what to think. She was so worried about DD, and now Karla is laying this on her! She became furious and backed away from Karla. Jane wondered as she glared at Karla if her friend really had something to do with George's death.

"Karla, I don't have time for your bummer shit. I can't think about George right now. DD is sick, and I need to get to her. Sorry, I asked you over. You can leave now." Jane cried as she turned away. She heard Karla slam the door behind her as she left.

CHAPTER 25

DD stayed home from school the rest of that week. Jane politely told her boss she couldn't come to work for a few days. DD swallowed the pills her mom gave her, 'like a big girl .'She drank lots of water and ate well. Jane made soup and a salad for her. They watched TV together almost all day in the beanbag chairs and then had grilled cheese sandwiches with carrot sticks for dinner.

"I feel better, Mommy. Can I go to school tomorrow? My headache went away." DD asked, hopefully at the end of the week as she was putting on her nightgown and thinking about school. Dandelion loved school and being with all of her friends. She didn't want to have to stay home another day.

"Yeah, sweetie, the doctor said if you feel well enough to go, you could. On Monday, though, tomorrow is Saturday." Jane smiled with a sigh of relief, thinking maybe everything was all right after all. She still didn't have those test results, but watching DD feel so much better gave Jane hope.

Grampa picked up DD after school on Monday. When he asked how she was, she told him she had a headache. "But don't tell mommy, she cried last time I had a headache." DD didn't like to see her mother cry.

He assured DD she wouldn't have to go back to the hospital if she told Mommy and that Mommy would just give her a pill to make the headache go away. "Don't worry, mommies cry all the time; they worry and fret about everything. You will, too, someday when you are a mommy." Grampa told his little granddaughter.

DD giggled.

Her dad told Jane about the headache when she got home from work, and she rushed into the living room, where DD was lying down on the couch.

"Are you okay? Does your head still hurt?" She gently rubbed her hand across DD's forehead, checking for a fever. She wasn't warm.

"Take this pill. The doctor said you could take these pills whenever you had a headache." She handed DD a glass of water with the Tylenol.

DD took the pill from her mother's hand and swallowed it. She smiled and said, "Like a big girl". Then she lay back on the couch again, cuddling up in the blanket Grampa gave her.

When Jane's dad came into the kitchen, she yelled at him. "Why didn't you call me? You have to call me when something is wrong! You know that!"

"I didn't even know. Not until I picked her up after school!" He yelled back, "Besides, it's just a regular headache; she isn't throwing up, and it doesn't feel like she has a fever."

"But you should have called me, Dad, so I could come home," Jane raged. She discussed this with him that very morning.

"Why, so you could look at her? There's nothing you could do, Jane, and I'm here with her, aren't I?" He was getting upset. He understood Jane's frustration. He was frustrated, too, but tried to stay calm for DD's sake. He knew she could hear them.

DD yelled to her mom, "I feel better, don't fight." She felt like it was her fault and cried, which didn't help her headache any.

Jane came into the living room and sat down by DD. "I know I shouldn't be upset, but Dandelion, I love you and want to make you all better. I just don't know how." Tears rolled down her face.

"Go to the park. I want to go to the park, Mommy." DD looked at her mom hesitantly. She knew her mom was always happy at the park.

117

Looking lovingly at her little girl, Jane replied, "No, DD, you have to rest until your headache goes away." At this time, DD lay back down and turned toward the TV. She fell asleep in a few minutes, and Jane left the room.

Back in the kitchen, her dad was getting his coat on to leave, and Jane said, "I'm sorry, Dad, that I yelled at you. I hate waiting to hear about test results. Why can't they just tell you right away when it's something like this?" He agreed.

Jane wiped the tears off her cheek and hugged her dad. "I think I WILL go to the park. That was a good suggestion from DD. Will you stay for a while and watch her for me? She's asleep. I won't stay long. I just need some space to think for a while." She smiled at him.

"Sure, I'll stay with DD." He slipped his coat back off.

"You go ahead and stay as long as you want. I think it'll be good for you. DD should sleep for a while now, and if I need you, I know where you are." He smiled back at her. She liked it when her dad smiled at her. Felt like love.

Jane put the thick shawl around her shoulders and grabbed a hat. She also grabbed the small box that held her smoke and put it in her beaded purse.

"Thank you, Dad." She said as she walked out the door.

CHAPTER 26

At the park, she went by the forget-me-nots, which were George's favorite flowers and picked herself a bouquet. Clinging tightly to the flowers, she looked up to the sky and asked, "Oh, God, if you are there, tell George that I love him and that I will always miss him. Oh, and God, or Jesus, whoever will listen, PLEASE take away our little star's headache and don't let anything be wrong with Dandelion. PLEEEASE, don't leave me with another lost love. PLEASE God, Jesus."

Jane climbed up on the train and got out of her box. She loaded her pipe with a pinch of grass and held it up high. "This one's for you, Georgie." She liked to remember him when she smoked grass because they always had such a good time smoking together. Their conversations would get deep, and they would always laugh a lot.

Before she took a second toke, she heard Karla say, "Your dad said I'd find you here. What's happenin', Jane?"

Jane angrily looked at Karla and asked, "What do you want?"

"I want to talk to you, Jane, about the other day." Karla was sincere.

"What about?" Jane pouted.

"George." Karla approached Jane hesitantly. "It's my fault."

Jane thought about this for a while before responding to Karla.

"Why is it your fault, Karla? Because you gave him those reds?"

Jane put another pinch of weed in her pipe and offered it to Karla, "Here, mellow out." Karla lit the pipe and held on to it for a while.

"So, Karla," Jane began after contemplating this story, "You think you are responsible for George's death?" She paused before saying, "I don't think so. We both know that George was wild about having fun, and we know he liked to party. If it hadn't been you, Karla, who gave him the reds, it would have been someone else; he was always looking for a way to get high. That was George. Right, Karla?"

"But I was the one." Karla insisted, sobbing, "I was the one."

"Hey Karla. George is the one who did it. " Jane sighed and took another toke off her pipe. "But I'm glad you didn't tell me when it happened 'cause I'd have never forgiven you back then. But I do forgive you now, Karla. I understand. Peace." She really did understand because she really did know George. She knew his wants and wild desires.

Then Jane hugged Karla. "You don't still, do you?" She asked, "Reds?"

"NO!" Karla yelled out, "I never do reds anymore!" She cried hard, "Oh George, I'm so sorry."

Later, when she gathered herself together, Karla asked Jane, "So why are you here and not at home with Dandelion?"

"I hate waiting, and I'm so worried. I worry that DD is going to have the same thing as my mom had and die like she did!" she became frantic again. "I wanted to get away and pray, yes, pray. It's that important." Jane was serious. "I already lost Mom, Irma, and George. I just CAN'T lose Dandelion. She's my whole world!"

Karla grabbed Jane by the shoulders, saying, "You don't know what it is yet, Jane. It could be just a headache. You know HEADACHE like normal people get?" Karla stared into Jane's eyes.

Then Karla hugged her, "Maybe the flu? That Hong Kong flu that was around a couple of years ago was a bad one, and it gave people bad headaches. Has she been checked for that?"

"I don't know what they're checking her for. They don't tell me anything, Karla." Jane sighed.

"Well, let's just say for now that DD has a headache due to the flu, so let it go." Karla again was serious.

Jane smiled at the thought and handed the pipe to Karla. "Well, I guess you could be right. I really DON'T know yet."

"Yeah," she coughed, "I think waiting is the way to go right now." She handed the pipe back to Jane.

They stayed on the train for a while and then took a long walk around the park, talking about anything BUT DD or George.

Jane eventually told Karla she should get back home to DD and asked her if she wanted to come over. They decided to meet at Jane's house. Karla would stop by the new little restaurant 'Taco Bell' on her way and pick up some tacos for dinner.

When Jane got home, her dad told her that DD was still asleep and didn't even miss her mommy. Jane thanked him again and gave him a hug when he left. Karla arrived with the tacos a few minutes later.

After they ate, Karla brought out a bottle of strawberry wine. Jane opened it and poured each of them a glass. DD whimpered in the living room, making Jane run to her.

"Mommy, my headache went away, and I'm hungry." DD looked at her mother wantingly, rubbing her belly.

"Well, guess what?" she smiled, "Aunt Karla brought us tacos. Do you want one?"

"YEAH!" DD climbed up to the table.

After she ate half a taco, DD went into her bedroom to play, telling her dolls all about her day, "I went to school and played with my friends, and the teacher was nice, but I got a headache and, shhh, don't tell mommy cause she will cry, and now I'm all better." DD dressed her doll in pajamas.

"More wine, Jane?" Karla asked.

"Right On. I'm feeling mellow. We might as well drink it up." Jane felt relaxed. It had been a hard few days waiting for results, but she knew she deserved to relax. Hoping tomorrow will bring the phone call with the results. She told Karla that maybe she should stay home from work to get the call. Karla assured her it would be "a damn good reason to miss work."

CHAPTER 27

Jane waited all morning by the phone, occasionally picking it up and listening for the dial tone to make sure it was working. When afternoon came, she went into the backyard to do some work, so she put the phone in the back window to be able to hear it if it rang. Her mind was wandering, and she couldn't keep it straight no matter what she tried. She raked some leaves and piled sticks here and there. She cried. Looking at the phone every ten minutes, checking it to see if it was off the hook. Jane waited. Pleading with the stars, God, the Whole Universe. She hated Leo again. Wishing for her Mother's help, wishing for George's comfort, Jane cried loudly as she watered the new bush.

When it was time to pick up DD from school, she asked her dad to get her so she wouldn't miss the phone call. Of course, Hank agreed. He came into the house when he brought DD home, asking Jane, "Hear anything?"

"Not yet," Jane answered harshly. She was mad.

The next day was her regular day off. Wishing she would have heard yesterday about the test results, Jane began cursing the doctor in her mind. She missed a day of work waiting for his call. What WAS he doing? Didn't he know she was waiting? A couple of hours later, the phone rang. Jane raced to answer it, "Hello…"

"Hello, I'd like to speak with Jane Volsandt."

"Yes, this is Jane."

"This is Dr. Litner's office calling regarding the tests Dandelion had a few days ago." She said it as if Jane would have forgotten about them.

"Yes, Yes, go on." Jane was waiting.

"The results seem to be okay, with no major problems; however, the doctor wants to do one more test on her. Can you bring her in tomorrow morning?"

"Yes, Yes, I can." Jane was relieved and scared at the same time. Another test, for what? The nurse didn't tell her. Was DD okay or not? She still didn't really know.

"Tomorrow, tomorrow. Shit!" She whispered to herself, anticipating another night of waiting. Another missed day of school for DD. She had to call work and miss another day, too. She was grateful that her boss knew what was going on. Her boss also had a little girl, so she understood Jane's concern.

But Jane still had to get through this day. What would she do? Work in the backyard some more? She tried that already. What? Why? Oh, the pain and misery of waiting! Jane slammed her fist on the table. Then she got out her pipe.

The next morning, on the way to the doctor's office, DD told her mother that she felt better. Jane told her she was going, whether she liked it or not. Her nerves were flaring up, and she tried to stay calm but somehow just couldn't get a grip.

When the doctor came into the office they were waiting in, he smiled and said, "Hello, Miss Jane and little Miss... flower ... " He was lost for the name, and Jane quickly said, "Dandelion. Dandelion Daisy Volsandt."

"Ah yes, I remember now. How are you two?"

"We are okay if DD is okay. What's happenin', Dr. Litner? Is DD okay? Does she have a tumor? Is she going to ...?" Tears filled Jane's eyes, and she turned her head.

"Yes, Jane, little Dandelion is fine," the doctor continued, "She had a touch of the Hong Kong flu. It was around a few years ago and made a comeback last year. It was a terrible flu, deadly. But Dandelion has defeated that. She has a good immune system."

124

Dr. Litner explained the flu symptoms to Jane, and she agreed that this was what DD had gone through. The vomiting and fever.

"However," Jane told the doctor, "she does still get headaches. She had one the other day again. She doesn't want to tell me about them, but I know she gets them. Why is that, Dr. Litner?" Jane wasn't sure her little girl was out of trouble yet.

"I have one more test for her right now, and you can come in with her if you want to, Jane. How about it?" The kind doctor smiled at both of them as he opened the door to the hallway.

Jane said okay and went down the hall, holding DD's hand and following the doctor into a darkened room. He sat Dandelion up on a chair with big machines attached to it and turned out the light. Then, a little light appeared down the wall, showing some letters.

DD immediately read the top letter, "That's an E over there." She giggled. The doctor said, "Good, now, read the next line." She had some trouble with that row, calling the 'r' a 't' and the 'a'

a 'c'. The next line she couldn't read at all. "I can't see those letters," DD told the doctor. She rubbed her eyes.

"What's wrong with her, Dr.?" Jane was sure that a tumor or something was blocking her vision.

The doctor cleared his throat and said, "Your little Dandelion needs glasses, Jane. She is getting headaches because she is straining her eyes at school. A nice pair of glasses should fix her up fine and 'DD'!" He smiled at the joke he just made, knowing how relieved Jane must be. Jane laughed.

"Just glasses? What were all those tests for then?"

"Well, I had to make sure that what I was thinking about the Hong Kong flu was correct, and I also had to rule out the same thing your mother had because I knew you would ask me about it," he said, "and I did. Little Miss Flower is healthy.

And I couldn't be happier for the two of you! You're a good mother, Jane."

They left the doctor's office laughing. DD was laughing at her mom, and Jane was laughing for relief. They danced all the way to the car grampa was waiting in.

"You need glasses, DD, you're fine." Jane laughed again.

When she told her dad the good news, he cried and confessed to Jane how worried he had been. They hugged.

One of the other kids in DD's class wore glasses, and DD had wondered why, but now she knew. "I'll wear glasses like my friend in school, Betty, huh, mommy?" she questioned.

"Yeah, we'll get you some of those wire-framed ones, oval or maybe round ones like John Lennon." Jane was so overjoyed about the good news that she twirled in a circle, holding DD's hands.

Karla stopped by as soon as they got home to find out the latest. "How's our little flower today?" She cutely asked, not wanting DD to know about her concern. Then she kissed the top of DD's head.

"She's fine, Karla, she's OKAY!" Jane answered happily.

"Outa-site!" Karla laughed, "Right on, sister."

Jane explained the Hong Kong flu to Karla, telling her she had the right diagnosis. Then shouted, "Now she needs GLASSES. Her eyes were giving her those headaches. No wonder she was having a hard time in school. She couldn't see the blackboard! And the beading I'm trying to teach her, that must be why she couldn't seem to do it." Jane beamed.

"And glasses will fix her. Isn't that great, Karla? Glasses!" Jane was elated. "The glasses should be ready next week. And DD is happy to get them. She will look so cute in the frames we picked out."

Karla hugged her and then hugged DD. Then they all hugged together, jumping up and down in a circle, laughing.

126

"Now, will YOU be okay, Mommy? When my headaches go away?" DD asked, hoping her mother was happy enough now to be her usual calm, loving self.

Jane and Karla both laughed.

"Yes, DD, my little star flower, yes, you and I both will be okay now. Mommy will smile like always… And once you get those cute glasses, you will be able to see really well, and your headaches WILL go away. I promise."

She gave her a hug so tight that DD squeaked out a little yell, "Mom-mee." Jane let her go and told her she loved her.

"I want to go outside and play with my dolls and tell them the good news. Mommy, can I go?" DD asked.

"Yes, Dandelion, you can go. I know your dolls have been worried about you." Jane giggled, "Stay in the fence."

"Okay, Mommy."

Karla and Jane sat at the kitchen table and sighed. Both were so relieved that neither of them knew what to say. They just sat there until Jane got out a bottle of wine. She poured them each a glass, which they drank after clinking a toast. Jane's dad walked in. "Celebrating the good news, Karla?"

"Yes, sir!" Karla replied with her usual salute. "Want to join us?"

"No, thanks. I have more important matters to tend to. Now, where is the cutest flower of the bunch?" Hank asked.

"She's outside, telling her dolls the good news."

"Well, I have to go get her. I want to take her out to celebrate. Maybe we'll go get ice cream!" He was happier than Jane ever remembered him being.

Jane went for DD, who was talking to her make-believe dog, that big old rock named Spot. She had her dolls sitting next to it as she told them the story of her headaches. DD came running when she found out that Grampa was there.

"Grampa, I need glasses just like Betty. And Mommy isn't crying anymore." DD jumped into his arms.

127

"I'm so happy for you, DD! What every good news reporter needs is ice cream. How 'bout it, let's go out for ice cream?" He smiled at his precious Grand Dandelion.

"Yay, Grampa, and me, are going out to get ice cream, Mommy. Want to go?" DD was skipping toward the front door.

"No, DD, Mommy's tired. You go with Grampa and have a fun time, okay? I love you." She gave her a kiss as they left. Grampa and DD bounded out the door for their celebration, laughing all the way.

CHAPTER 28

Jane poured another glass of wine for Karla and herself. They sat at the table smiling and talked about how her dad was so good with DD and how Hank had changed from drowning in alcohol.

"DD saved his life. He loves her like he used to love me." Jane told Karla. "Before my mom died." She looked up.

Karla commented, "We all know now that living through a death can really destroy someone. I understand your dad, Jane."

"Yeah, and now that he's not drinking as much, he seems to have a purpose in life." Jane understood, too. "DD is that purpose."

They both concluded that he needed DD to fix what was wrong with him. And hopefully, he wouldn't drown in alcohol anymore. Jane explained to Karla how she would feel lost without her dad in her life now. Of everyone she ever loved, he used to be the least, and right now, he was the most important.

Another glass of wine, the end of this bottle, and the two friends continued gabbing happily. They discussed Irma and her, 'I told you so.' And the many good times together with her.

Karla talked about a new friend who was a boy, "We are getting along great and even smoking together sometimes. He works near me, and I see him at the coffee shop in the mornings and after work. What do you call someone like this? He's not my boyfriend." Karla considered this. "Just plain friend, I guess. Who's a boy? What'd you call George?" she asked Jane. "Besides Georgie, I mean."

"Brother, he was my brother; my buddy, my best friend, but most of all, I called him brother." Jane smiled, looking at the poster of George hanging on the wall, pointing to it. She touched her heart.

"Well, Kevin and I aren't that close, so I guess 'friend' will have to do … for now …" She winked at Jane, making her laugh.

Jane knew how Karla liked boys with all they had to offer. Who knows? Jane thought that Kevin might just be Karla's next boyfriend by next week, in the full sense of the word. She chuckled silently to herself. Hopeful, Jane quietly prayed for Karla.

Jane hugged Karla when she left and then plopped down into her favorite chair. She sat there, feeling the soft mohair, thinking about all the turmoil her worrying had caused and how she should have had faith; after all, it goes along with hope and love.

'Faith, Hope and Love'. She had the floral poster in her living room. She just never knew who to have faith in. Now she knew. It was Jesus because he was the only one who ever answered her prayers.

She looked up and sighed, "Thank you, Jesus, for saving my little girl from a terrible tumor. Thank you for making her well. Thank you for hearing me pray. I guess you are real, after all. Someday, maybe you can explain to me about my mother, Irma, and George?"

She ended with, "Well, anyway, Peace and Love to you, Jesus."

Then she sat in her chair for a long while meditating.

Afterward, Jane got up and turned on the stereo. She went for the box on top of the refrigerator that held the pipe George made and her stash. She loaded the pipe, admiring its beauty once again, and lit the candle. Looking up to the ceiling as if through it to the sky, Jane said, "This one's for you, Georgie." The Beatles 'Good Day Sunshine' was playing on the radio. "But you know what, Georgie? I'm not going to smoke it this time." Jane turned the radio up loud and sighed heavily. "You wouldn't want me to, not now. Not anymore… right, Georgie? For our DD." Jane realized her worth, and she knew George was talking to her heart.

'Good – Day - Sunshine …' She sang along loudly as she put the pipe back into the box, returning it to its place on top of the fridge. Jane blew out the candle and thought of her little Dandelion Daisy as she sat back down in her big, comfy chair. Her very own little girl, just like her mother, had… full of love and adoration. Her very own living flower. She wanted to savor every moment with her. Every day for the rest of her life. The name 'Star Flower' floated into Jane's head, and she remembered George with so much love and appreciation.

"My very own piece of love, my own slice of Heaven." She smiled as she looked skyward and proclaimed with a heavy sigh,

"True Love, And it's Free, Imagine That".

Made in the USA
Coppell, TX
08 July 2024

34412465R00075